Praise for *Panic Peak*

Come for the story and stay for the science in this chilling cli-fi thriller. It's fascinating how Liggett weaves the two together. I couldn't put *Panic Peak* down.
—Margaret Mizushima, author of the award-winning Timber Creek K-9 Mysteries, including *Standing Dead*

A must read for anyone curious about the science of geoengineering and its potential impact on our world. This novel seamlessly blends entertainment and thrill with education. The characters' journeys unfold against a backdrop of scientific exploration and ethical dilemmas, offering a unique perspective that engages both the lay reader and the scientifically inclined.
—Radwiga (Yaga) Richter, PhD, Special Projects Lead to the National Center for Atmospheric Research (NCAR) Director

This sequel to *Watermelon Snow* is an engaging plot-driven thriller that pits two climate scientists against each other, leading to a regional climate catastrophe, danger, and death. By the third chapter, I was hooked and could not put my iPad down.
—Judith Auer, DMA, Performer/Professor/Stage Director

Liggett's novel about geoengineering is both informative and engaging. The concern that this story raises about illegal weather modification is quite realistic. The setting in the Pacific Northwest is a good place for cloud seeding. Snow is already abundant in that region, and cloud seeding is designed to increase the efficiency of what is already occurring naturally. I found the story scientifically credible and stimulating at the same time.
—Roy Rasmussen, PhD, Senior Scientist, Hydrometeorological Applications Program, National Center for Atmospheric Research (NCAR)

PANIC PEAK

PANIC PEAK

A CLI-FI THRILLER

WILLIAM A. LIGGETT

Consilience Press LLC
Niwot, Colorado

Panic Peak
William A. Liggett
Copyright © 2024 by William A. Liggett

Print ISBN: 979-8-9899544-0-7
Ebook ISBN: 979-8-9899544-1-4
LCCN: 2024902064

Cp

Consilience Press LLC
Niwot, Colorado
www.consiliencepress.com

Coaching and editing by Laurel Kallenbach, www.laurelkallenbach.com
Editing by Melanie Mulhall, Dragonheart, www.TheDragonheart.com
Publishing Services: Journey Bound Publishing,
www.JourneyBoundPublishing.com

Front cover photo of Panic Peak: Adam Walker, used by permission
(Panic Peak, Olympic National Park, Washington)

First Edition
Printed in the United States of America

For Cathy, my wife,
whose friendship spans decades.

Blue Glacier Research Station – University of Washington

1

Olympic Peninsula, Washington State

Monday, October 5

As Kate sped in her car from Seattle, the dark clouds became more threatening. Halfway to her meeting at the Hoh Rainforest Visitor Center on the west side of the Olympic Peninsula, the rain, now a downpour, pounded on her windshield. She drove as fast as she dared but was careful to avoid hydroplaning. As she scanned for the sign pointing to the Hoh Rainforest, frequent bolts of lightning flashed, lighting up the otherwise dark-gray sky. Even with the windshield wipers on high, she strained to see. She couldn't remember a time when she'd experienced such heavy rain in her nearly ten years of living in the Pacific Northwest.

Minutes later, she flew right past the Hoh Rainforest turnoff and didn't dare slam on the brakes. Instead, she crept down the highway until she found a pullout where she turned around and headed back, craning her neck to see through her blurry windshield.

The narrow side road cut through dense forest bounded by trees on both sides. It was so dark that Kate felt she was driving at midnight instead of one thirty in the afternoon. The trees were shrouded with dripping moss, dangling from branches like a forest surrounding a haunted house. Kate felt she couldn't take her eyes off the road even for a second, and her hands ached from gripping the steering wheel. She passed a wall of sandbags on her right that held back an expanse of water. The Hoh River threatened to swallow the road. Kate hoped this meeting would be worth the hair-raising drive.

That morning, she'd received a text from Ben Johnson, a national park ranger friend. It read, "Urgent: Dept. of Interior meeting this afternoon to approve demolition of Blue Glacier Research Station. Can you testify? Last chance."

She'd been about to begin a lecture to her morning class on retreating glaciers at the University of Washington when the text came in, and she pivoted quickly to ask her teaching assistant to take over the class. On her walk back to her office, she called Ben, and he answered immediately.

"Kate, I'm sorry for the short notice. The Department of the Interior has added your research station on Mount Olympus to a list of structures to be torn down. Management has decided to eliminate buildings it considers nonessential from national parks. Apparently, your research station falls in that category."

"Typical bureaucrats." Kate spat out the words, having little patience for those who didn't value science. "When did you find out?"

"Just this morning, and the final decision is this afternoon. I can have one witness to try to change their minds, and you've taught more students from that station than anyone. They use a secure Defense Department connection, a system called NiPRnet, to prevent security breaches. You'll have to come here. We have an authorized sign-on."

"That's a five-hour drive, Ben, and it's raining here. It's probably worse where you are."

"We're last, starting at five eastern time, so you'll have time to make the drive. It's your only chance to prevent the station's destruction."

Kate thought about all the summers she'd led graduate student research teams from that station. "I'll do it. This is too important."

As she pulled into the visitor center parking lot, the rain fell in torrents, and thick clouds obscured the tops of the giant conifers that towered over the small building huddled at their base. Kate slung her messenger bag over her shoulder and cracked open the door enough to poke her umbrella through. She popped open the umbrella, slid out of the car, and dashed across the parking lot, sloshing through a half inch of water and soaking her socks.

The umbrella offered little protection, and by the time she reached the door, her hair, jacket, and jeans were dripping. She was dressed for a university class, not a meeting with Washington, DC, muckety-mucks in suits and ties, and now she was a cold, wet mess.

Well, she thought, this is what a climate researcher looks like, more often than not. Maybe the disheveled look would work in her favor.

She opened the glass door and dropped her umbrella in the entryway. While striding over to the counter toward Ranger Ben, she shook water off her head and ran her fingers through her sopping hair.

Shivering and soaked, she waited impatiently while Ben argued with a man and woman who seemed determined to go hiking, even though the trails were closed. Ben kept pointing at the chalkboard by the main desk, where someone had written "Trails closed: hazardous conditions." Two children wandered through the gift shop. The girl, who appeared to be about eight, picked up a fuzzy bear and hugged it while the boy, about twelve, gawked at his smartphone.

The man looked angry and said in a loud voice, "This is a rainforest. It's supposed to rain."

"You *must* leave the park immediately," Ben told the parents. "The road's about to flood."

Still looking angry but also slightly alarmed, the couple finally turned and herded the kids out the door.

Ben looked over at Kate and motioned for her to come around the counter to join him.

"Am I too late?" She removed her dripping jacket and looked up at him. "If you hadn't sent the text, I wouldn't have even known about this meeting."

Ben glanced at the wall clock. "We still have fifteen minutes." He took her jacket and handed her a towel. "Thanks for coming."

"I got here as fast as I could. I just need to use the restroom."

In the lady's room mirror, Kate flinched when she saw how her short, blonde hair was plastered to her head in random swirls. She dried her hair with the towel Ben had given her and used a brush from her purse to create the approximation of a professional look. As she inspected her appearance, she was grateful she had no makeup to smear and run. Her suntan from hiking the glacier weeks before gave her face a healthy glow, and her slender figure reflected her time climbing and regular workouts during the academic year. So much was riding on this meeting that she hoped she looked the part of an experienced professor in her early thirties and not one of her students. Taking the opportunity to warm up, she stood in front of the mirror and recited the opening lines she'd been practicing since leaving Seattle.

After Kate returned, Ben said, "You'll have five minutes to testify." Ushering her to a chair at the table, he then pulled up another chair next to hers and opened his laptop.

"As I was driving," Kate said, "I tried to organize my thoughts. Any suggestions?"

"Science. Some on the panel might be sympathetic to science, so you might try to convince them." Looking somewhat distracted while logging in to the conference, he added, "You'll do great."

Kate watched as the host introduced the committee members, two men and two women. Kate didn't recognize any of them. One was a recent political appointee whose views on climate change might become apparent during the course of the hearing. The other three were career employees she thought might have science backgrounds. They all looked exhausted after sitting through a full day of testimony with hers being their last.

When Ben introduced Kate, she saw the members sit up a little, maybe curious to have someone testifying who was not in the Park Service. Feeling emotion rising in her chest as she recalled the faces of the many students she'd exposed to the world of snow and ice on Blue Glacier, Kate leaned in toward the camera on Ben's laptop and began. "I recognize that our station is an artificial structure overlooking Blue Glacier. I respect your goal to return the parks to their natural states. However, please consider the scientific research and careers of young scholars seeking answers to global warming. These engaged students will be the scientists of tomorrow. It's critical that they have the chance to study a living glacier—while there still is one."

She cleared her throat while she steadied her voice. "This historic station has been in this location since the International Geophysical Year in 1957. Its existence allows us to maintain the continuity of data for decades while revealing the impact of global warming. Our landmark station permits the scientific study of climate at the heart of one of America's premier national parks. No other park—not Glacier, not Rocky Mountain—has an alpine glacier the size of Blue Glacier with the facilities already in place to support a program of research."

A member of the panel raised his hand. "Dr. Landry, can you provide our committee with publications that you and your former students have produced based on your work on the glacier?"

Kate breathed a quiet sigh of relief and nodded at Ben. At least one committee member was listening thoughtfully. "Chief Ranger Johnson is uploading a list of publications now."

Another member of the panel asked, "Why can't you simply fly your students and equipment to the glacier each summer?"

"Good question! The cost and living conditions would make that approach impractical. Studying climate twenty-four seven requires a fixed base, such as the research station, where instruments can be installed, stored, and—"

Suddenly, an amplified male voice blared from a handheld transceiver on the table, startling Kate. "Ranger Johnson, Clark here. We've got a serious problem."

Ben grabbed the radio and brought it to his mouth. "Tell me, Clark."

"The Hoh River breached our levee. The road is swamped. It's impassable. Any visitors still there?" The alarm in the guy's voice was unmistakable.

"The last ones here were a family, but they left. It's just me and Dr. Landry," Ben said.

"The water's covering the road. Never seen it this high. Better come take a look."

Ben addressed the committee. "I apologize. We've got an urgent situation here I must deal with."

The host of the panel said, "Ben, we understand. Dr. Landry, we appreciate the description of your station's contribution to the national park and science. I think we've heard enough to make our decision."

Kate began, "But I wanted to say—"

Ben slammed his laptop shut, snatched the radio, and stood. "Kate, come with me."

Kate felt frustrated to be cut short, but she was worried too. "Has the road flooded this fast before?"

"Never." Ben grabbed his raincoat and hat from a hook on the wall and strode through the lobby, Kate scrambling to keep up. As they approached the front door, a flash of light filled the room and a thunderous boom shook the building. The lightning hit a nearby tree, raining debris on a white sedan just as it raced from the parking lot.

"That's the family," Ben shouted. He ran out the door waving his arms. "Stop! The road's closed." As the car sped past, he turned to Kate. "We've got to stop them."

They sprinted to the truck parked nearby, splashing through puddles now up to their ankles, and Ben started the engine, turning on flashing lights and the siren.

The car had a head start, and they couldn't catch it, given the slick pavement. Rounding a blind curve, Kate saw the flashing red lights on a second Park Service truck parked off the pavement close to the water's edge, and Ben slid to a stop.

Up ahead, the brake lights on the family's sedan flashed just as it skidded sideways and flew into the river, skipping like a flat rock over the surface. Kate sat stunned. "Oh . . . my . . . God!"

Ben jumped out of the truck. "Stay here!" Then, turning back through the open door, he pointed to the radio on the dash and said, "Call headquarters. Tell them we need search and rescue." He slammed the door and ran to the water's edge.

Kate picked up the microphone and fumbled with the radio knobs. The backlit display read "Channel 3," telling her the radio was powered on. She pushed the button on the microphone. "Mayday, Mayday. Is anyone receiving me?"

A male voice came on. "This is Ranger Lopez, Olympic Park headquarters. Who is this? What's happened?"

"This is Dr. Kate Landry. Ranger Ben Johnson asked me to call for search and rescue. I'm in his truck about five miles from the Hoh Rainforest Visitor Center. The Hoh River has flooded the road and a passenger car just skidded and flew into the water." While she was talking, Kate watched Ben wade into the river up to his knees and then return to shore, head hanging and shoulders drooping. "The car is too far out and floating downstream. Oh, my God. Send someone. Hurry!"

As Kate looked helplessly through the windshield, she glimpsed the shape of a child's face in the car's side window, mouth open in a scream. The car sailed away, swept into the middle of the roiling river. Kate gasped and held her breath as the car sank to the windows and rolled slowly to one side.

Kate was frozen—watching, praying—until there was no longer any sign of the car or the family trapped inside. She heard muffled voices as Ben talked to the other ranger.

Ben opened the door and climbed behind the wheel next to Kate. "You call for search and rescue?"

"Yes. But we haven't heard back."

After calling on the radio to confirm that help was on the way, Ben used his hand to wipe the condensation off the inside of his windshield. "You'll need to stay with Alice and me tonight."

Kate was too stunned to answer.

"Kate, did you hear me?"

Nodding slowly, she said, "I don't know what to do next."

"Yeah, we'll figure it out."

"I need to go back to the visitor center and pack up my things."

He shook his head. "Your stuff is fine. The building's secure. Let's just go." He shifted into gear and turned back toward the visitor center and ranger housing.

"I keep replaying it over and over in my mind," Kate said. She squeezed her eyes shut as if that would purge the memory of what seemed to be a child's face.

"I know." He paused, and she looked over at him to see him staring straight ahead. "Someone needs to do something about global warming. And this extreme weather," he finally muttered.

2

MGM Grand Hotel, Las Vegas, Nevada

Tuesday, October 6

Dr. Mark Cooper had long felt he could be the man who solved global warming. Now he was sure of it. This all-day meeting had been the most productive one he'd had in his quarter-century career as a scientist. His audience, a secretive cartel, consisted of ten of the most powerful and wealthy oil company executives in the world. They treated him with deference and showed the respect for his life's work it deserved.

Facing them, Cooper stood to the side of a projection screen hanging from the ceiling in the wood-paneled executive conference room on the top floor of the hotel. Floor-to-ceiling tinted windows behind the men seated at the table framed the stark desert landscape outside. An armed security guard was stationed outside the open doorway, something unthinkable back at his university.

He projected the image of snow-covered mountains in Wyoming. "Cloud seeding has increased snowfall in this location by as much as ten percent. We can expect at least this much on Mount Olympus."

A stocky man seated at the table raised his hand. "If my calculations are correct, Dr. Cooper, that would add about twenty feet of additional snow to Blue Glacier."

"Exactly. And that's only part of the operation. I will be using commercial aircraft to cool the atmosphere, and here's a blueprint of the boats I will deploy west of the Olympic Peninsula." He projected a diagram of what appeared to be a commercial fishing boat. "The powerful pumps hidden in this vessel will spray seawater into the clouds overhead, causing more frequent storms."

He heard whispers of "brilliant" and "innovative" as the men turned to one another.

"The key to changing the climate will be the combined effect of all these components operating simultaneously. This has never been done, but I'm confident it will work."

The leader of the group, known to all as "Tex," stood his full six feet, three inches and addressed the others in his distinctive twang. "Gentlemen, I for one am convinced that Dr. Cooper's plan will deliver what we've been looking for. The daily drumbeat in the media about man-made climate change is beginning to build a political consensus to reduce oil and gas production. Our highly paid consultants and lobbyists are no longer as effective in generating confusion and doubt in people's minds as they once were. Dr. Cooper's technology can lower temperatures around the world, masking the warming from fossil fuels and allowing us to continue oil production indefinitely."

"I'm particularly interested in his idea of adding sulfur to jet fuel," a cartel member from a Brazilian company said. "That's something we can control with our distribution channels." Several of the men nodded their agreement.

Another member raised his hand and spoke with a thick Russian accent. "I move we cover Dr. Cooper's start-up costs, as he requested, and pay the remaining compensation contingent upon his attaining his targets for cooling Mount Olympus this year." The others voiced their agreement.

Cooper was ecstatic and beamed as he shook hands around the table, and Tex handed him a wire transfer receipt covering the cartel's initial payment. Then Cooper shoved his laptop and papers into his briefcase and hurried to leave the hotel and its noisy slot machines to catch his flight to LA. He looked forward to returning to the quiet of his lab at Caltech where, surrounded by scientific instruments and equipment, the creative ideas came to him almost as easily as breathing air.

Just as he reached the conference room door, Faisal Abadi, the cartel member from Saudi Arabia, stopped him. "Dr. Cooper, may I have a word?"

"I've got a plane to catch." Well over six feet, Cooper towered over Faisal, who was short but built like a tank.

"This will just take a minute. I was impressed with your plan. It's quite brilliant."

"Thanks." Cooper's strained smile reflected his eagerness to get going.

Faisal's eyes narrowed. "But you failed to convince some of us of your ability to protect our operation from being detected once you've implemented it. Our investment in you will be worse than wasted if word of this becomes public."

Cooper glanced around the room and noticed the others watching him attentively. Embarrassed and annoyed, he couldn't let this confrontation tarnish the success he'd achieved. "You've already made that clear."

Faisal reached out and squeezed Cooper's arm with vice grip force. "Let me add, then, that we will hold you personally accountable for any leaks. There will be a price to pay."

Cooper tried to pull away from the painful grip. "I take that as a threat." Cooper could feel his face growing warm as he spoke.

"If you trust me to implement the plan, you must trust me with the security of that plan."

Still latched on Cooper's arm, Faisal said, "The threat, my friend, is to emphasize my point. Be careful. Do you understand what I'm telling you?"

"Everything's been taken care of. Now I really must go."

Faisal released his grip but not his gaze. "Peace be with you, my friend."

Cooper didn't reply and noticed the others still watching as he charged out the door. He rushed down the hall, wondering if he had gotten into something more dangerous than he'd realized.

After catching the hotel shuttle and jogging through the terminal, Cooper barely got on the plane before the door closed. He sat back in his first-class seat, trying to relax by listening to his favorite Bach prelude on his headset, but Faisal's words about paying the price if he failed to maintain the security of the project brought to mind all sorts of grisly scenarios. These guys in thousand-dollar suits had the resources to do a lot worse than fund an unsanctioned science experiment. The thought left him unnerved.

The flight attendant offered a complimentary drink, and he requested a strong one: whiskey on the rocks.

Thank goodness Tex and the others weren't afraid to support his proposal for cooling the planet. Every group he'd pitched to before—NOAA, the National Science Foundation, and the American Meteorological Society—turned him down because Congress had cut funding for climate research. And even though they didn't say so, he suspected that one reason those organizations rejected his proposals was fear of lawsuits. People might blame them for floods or drought, regardless of whether he had caused them. In desperation, Cooper had looked for unconventional ways to fund his inventions.

How ironic that he'd found support from oil men who wanted to continue selling a product that contributed to the very problem he wanted to solve. He felt vindicated, but more than that. He now had the resources he needed to save humanity. His ultimate goal, to reverse global warming by extracting carbon dioxide from the atmosphere, required a massive infusion of cash.

Cooper dragged his briefcase out from under the seat in front of him and retrieved the wire transfer receipt. It showed the first installment toward the cartel's ultimate financial commitment: more money than the gross national product of some small countries. He smiled and sipped his drink in celebration.

He looked out the window at the sea of lights as they descended into the Los Angeles Basin. The short flight was almost over, yet he kept thinking of the meeting. "Our goal is to get environmentalists off our backs," the men in the cartel had said. "Just deploy your technology to create regions of cooling. We can publicize those as examples to offset headlines about steadily rising temperatures."

Their motivation was questionable, but he could live with that. It was exciting to have his ideas met with approval instead of the skepticism he was used to. No way would he let Faisal's threat ruin this day of triumph.

3
Kate Landry's Condo
Seattle, Washington

Tuesday, October 6

Grant had heard nothing from Kate since her call the night before. Knowing she was safe at Ben's house was both a relief and a concern. Though he knew she was in good hands with Ben and was relieved the flooding hadn't been bad enough to engulf the visitor center or Ben's residence, he also knew her tendency was to act first and question the wisdom of it later. He was somewhat annoyed that she'd taken the risky drive into the heavy rain and flood conditions. And this was the first time they'd spent a night apart since they'd begun sharing Kate's apartment two months earlier.

They had met that June when Grant flew to Blue Glacier under a NASA grant to observe Kate's research team as they collected data in the isolated mountainous setting. She had a reputation for forming a cohesive graduate student team in a short time. How she managed that would be useful for NASA crews to learn in preparation for future space missions. The main research focus that summer for Kate and her students was the recovery of a prehistoric carcass they had discovered frozen in the glacier ice. Tragically, it contained a virus that was thought to have led to the death of two of her students and her pilot. Kate and Grant had escaped the illness, but it forced them to leave the glacier early.

Grant had taken an unpaid leave of absence from his faculty position at the University of California because he thought the climate crisis required more from him than he could give teaching. His time on the glacier had inspired him to tackle climate change, and he fell in love with Kate at the same time.

When his cell phone buzzed, he snatched it off the table. "Kate! Are you okay?"

"Grant, yes. I'm coming home. The rain stopped as Ben said it might. They cleared tons of mud from the road, so now it's passable."

"I've missed you. How long will it take to get here?"

"Without rain, about five hours."

"Drive safely."

Grant sat at the dining table waiting for Kate with his tall, lanky frame bent over the papers spread out in front of him. He flipped his hair away from his face as he took notes, but his concern about Kate made the hours go slowly. As he waited, he took breaks by taking walks around the block. Then he read the same climate research articles over and over again each time he returned.

Snowflake, Kate's cat, purred and nuzzled against his leg, leaving long, white hairs on his jeans. Grateful for the feline company, he bent down to rub her head, then straightened when he heard Kate's key in the lock. Both he and Snowflake jumped up to greet her, and when the door opened, he ushered her inside with a giant sigh of relief.

"I'm so glad you're home." He gave her a kiss, which she returned, putting both arms around him and squeezing.

She petted Snowflake and sat down on the couch, patting a cushion for Grant to join her. When he did, she grabbed his hand.

"The last eighteen hours have been hell. The white-knuckle drive to Ben's was awful. Then to see that family drown. Oh, Grant, I felt helpless." Tears ran down her cheeks.

Grant held her close and felt his own tears blur his vision. Kate's experience was personal, and it fueled his determination to push back against climate change and man's dependency on fossil fuels. "What do you think was causing the heavy rain? Do you think it was climate change?"

"Likely, but it's strange. The Hoh River floods occasionally, but never like that. And it seemed to be concentrated on the Olympic Peninsula, like it was in the bull's-eye for the storms. Ben says they've been coming every few days. Intense but then dissipating quickly."

Grant saw himself as rational and cautious, but he had just taken an unpaid leave of absence from his faculty position teaching social psychology and leadership at the University of California, Santa Cruz to stay with Kate. He knew he wanted to fight climate change in some way, but he wasn't sure how. This spontaneity was new to him.

"Didn't you check the weather before leaving for the Rainforest?" he asked cautiously.

"Of course I did. I knew it was raining hard, but I had no choice. I had to convince the Park Service not to tear down our research station."

He squeezed her shoulder. "It's just that I've occasionally seen you putting yourself in danger, and whenever you do, I worry." Kate's safety felt like his responsibility now, even though he knew at some level it really wasn't. He knew his anxiety stemmed from the loss of his fiancée in a boating accident two years earlier. He felt he might have saved her if only he'd gone sailing when she asked him to. And despite the fact that Kate was strong and responsible, even if a bit too willing to take chances, he couldn't shake his tendency to overreact whenever she was in potential danger.

Kate's eyes narrowed, telling Grant he'd made his point. She looked exhausted, and her face was drained of color, which didn't surprise Grant after all she'd been through. He stood and held out his hand, pulling Kate to her feet. His eyes went from her blonde hair to her blue eyes and then to her freckled nose.

When he planted a warm kiss on her lips, she answered with a passionate kiss and lingering embrace. Even though she'd only been gone two days, he'd missed her closeness and the way she slept with Snowflake curled around her shoulder. Guiding her gently toward the bedroom, he looked over his shoulder to see her smiling as she followed his lead.

4

Kate Landry's Condo

Wednesday, October 7 through Wednesday, October 14

Kate was half awake when Grant got dressed quietly and went out the front door. A half hour later she heard him fumbling with the lock. She opened the door wearing her bathrobe and put out her leg to block the cat from bolting.

Grant kissed her as he entered carrying a cup of coffee in each hand and a paper bag.

"It looks like you've been busy, Dr. Behavioral Scientist. Planning how to tackle climate change?" Kate asked as he cleared a space for the two of them at the dining table, which was cluttered with papers and books, as well as his laptop.

He said, "I'm logging all the climate-related articles I find every day in magazines, newspapers, and online publications. There are way too many to digest at one time. So I've created a database that I can sort by categories like extreme weather, sea level rise, and wildfires. This paper version represents a sample of them." He pointed to pieces of paper taped together.

"A kind of content analysis."

"Exactly. I'm focused on how climate news impacts our attitudes and actions. For every ten stories that document climate disasters, there's one that presents a potential solution, like carbon dioxide removal and storage. I've highlighted those solutions in green."

"Lots fewer of those," Kate said, spreading cream cheese on a bagel she'd snagged from the bag while studying the chart.

"Yes, and attitude studies have shown that people get discouraged when presented with problems over and over again with few or no solutions."

Kate nodded. "I've got to admit, it seems overwhelming. What do you think *you* can do?"

Grant cleared his throat. "I've been wondering how I, as a behavioral scientist, could help reduce global warming."

"I've been wondering the same thing," she said with a grin. She knew that Grant's brief but intense time on the rapidly shrinking Blue Glacier had shifted his priorities from teaching social psychology to climate change. But she also knew he needed to make a living and had been struggling with reconciling the two things. "Any ideas?"

"I need to study climate science to have any credibility and to influence people's actions."

Kate swiveled and looked him in the eye. "Are you serious? You don't need to go back to school. You spent years getting your PhD. There are already plenty of climate scientists documenting the threats."

"True. Just look at the number of articles I've found." He waved his hand over the spreadsheet.

"Do you know how many social psychologists are working on the problem? Not many, I bet." Kate paused while she organized her thoughts. "When it comes right down to it, the problem isn't the climate science. We've got that covered. Climate change is a *human* problem. We need to get the attention of humanity and get people, from individuals to governments, to make solving the climate crisis their number one priority." She scanned his face. "You *already* have the skills to make that happen."

Grant's half smile told her she was getting through to him. "Kate, you've got a point. I can only think of a handful of psychologists studying climate action. I could make a difference, but where to start?" He stared at his spreadsheet. "What's needed is a paradigm shift."

She nodded and moved her chair closer. "People use that term a lot, but what would it look like?"

"The current paradigm for reversing climate change is the belief that a knowledge deficit needs to be filled—that people need to be informed. The assumption is that people would act to correct the problem if they only knew that climate change is causing extreme weather. Actually, surveys have shown that about three-quarters of Americans already believe the climate is changing. They just don't know what to do about it."

He pointed to the rows of green. "These solutions are encouraging and offer hope in spite of the challenges ahead. They demonstrate that mankind is capable of mitigating global warming. It doesn't mean solutions are easy or that the problems can be ignored."

Kate grinned. "What you're saying is the media is using the old paradigm—trying to convince people that climate change is happening when most people already know it. But neither the media nor the general public are very aware of the many solutions being tested and deployed."

"Exactly. The new paradigm would be to foster realistic hope. Studies have shown this motivates people to take action, and hope provides a powerful force for change if people are aware that the problems are big and need more resources to solve them." Grant began talking faster. "It turns out, someone has already published a book that summarizes many of the solutions." He picked up a thick paperback and handed it to Kate. "It's called *Refresh: The Most Complete Guide to Restoring a Healthy Planet.* I don't have to reproduce this detailed inventory. I can use it as the basis for motivating people with hope instead of fear."

"I want to hear more about this. Let's go for a walk and you can tell me."

———

Throughout the following week Grant searched for job postings online and in professional journals, looking for something that would use his training and provided a way to instill hope and motivation for addressing climate. He knew it was not going to be easy and was about to stop his job search when he came across an ad for a position at the National Center for Atmospheric Research—NCAR—the number one spot for climate studies.

The job posting was for a PhD behavioral scientist to leverage existing and emerging solutions to global warming. They wanted someone who could develop a strategy to address the climate crisis that included individuals, corporations, and public entities. This fit perfectly with his skills as a social psychologist and even pointed to his focus on solutions.

The position was for one year as a visiting scientist, which was fine with Grant, who still had his position in Santa Cruz to fall back on. He was concerned, though, that it meant he and Kate would be apart for that year at a time when their relationship was just beginning. She encouraged him to apply and was confident they could stay connected through video calls and frequent trips. She thought it would be worth it for the future he wanted, as well as for their future together. Grant submitted an application, and a week later, he burst through the front door, his face lit with excitement.

"I got the job at NCAR! A job where I can make a difference!"

5

Dr. Cooper's Research Laboratory
California Institute of Technology

Wednesday, October 7

PhD candidate Samantha Schroeder stuffed an annoying strand of auburn hair behind her ear and peered into a sealed, clear plastic box that held a dozen shallow petri dishes. An opaque white ooze was forming on the surface of the minerals in each dish, and hoses circulated air containing a high level of carbon dioxide through the box.

She rolled up the sleeves of her lab coat and inserted her hands into the built-in rubber gloves on the side of the box. One at a time, she picked up the petri dishes and carefully weighed them on the digital scale inside the box, then called out the weights to Brad, her undergrad assistant, to record them in the research journal.

The weights were critical data for her dissertation on the geochemical process of converting atmospheric carbon dioxide to limestone. Her research was based on Dr. Cooper's theoretical analysis of a similar reaction that occurred naturally in places like Oman, in the Middle East where basaltic rocks exposed to the air formed limestone that removed carbon dioxide and trapped it permanently in solid form.

A man's voice boomed from behind her. "Calcite is condensing nicely, Sam."

She jumped, nearly dropping the petri dish she was holding. "Cooper! Jesus, you scared me." She withdrew her hands from the gloves and turned to glare at her advisor. "*Never* do that when I'm working! My PhD is riding on this data."

Cooper cocked his head and looked slightly rebuffed, but after a year of working with him, Sam knew he was secretly gloating that he'd riled her. She took a deep breath and adopted a more professional demeanor. "Sorry. I meant, 'Welcome back, Dr. Cooper. Brad and I weren't expecting to see you until next week.' But yes, our new catalyst is working fast. The higher carbon dioxide concentrations, like those in the atmosphere, create limestone even faster."

"Good work, you two." As Brad finished recording the weights, he added, "Brad, you can take a break for a few minutes. Sam, would you join me in my office?"

Brad left the room and Sam followed Cooper through the lab past floor-to-ceiling racks of electronic gear, which contained large display panels with flashing indicator lights that periodically emitted soft beeping tones. After more than a year of working here, she hardly noticed the sounds. She followed Cooper into his office, and he closed the door. Something was up. She could feel it.

She already knew that Cooper had arranged for a sabbatical from his Caltech lab to conduct field research and that the National Park Service had granted permission for him to fly equipment and supplies to a site on Blue Glacier because of his faculty position and Caltech's history of research there in the 1950s and '60s. But she knew nothing beyond that.

Cooper sat down. "I need your help."

She took the chair across from his desk and shrugged. "Okay. I've been wondering about your mystery project. All you ever say is that it involves geoengineering to cool the planet."

"I waited until I got funding to share the details with you. I need you to agree to strict confidentiality. Will you sign a nondisclosure agreement?"

"After more than a year you *still* don't trust me?"

"Calm down. This isn't up to me. The funding agency requires that everyone maintains complete secrecy. I *have* to ask you to sign this agreement before I can tell you the plan."

Sam drummed her fingers on the desk. "All right. Let me see it."

Cooper slid the agreement across his desk and handed her a pen. "It says nobody hears about this: not your boyfriend, not your mom, not your dog."

Sam rolled her eyes. "I don't have a boyfriend or a dog. And my mom lives over three hundred miles away." She uncapped the pen, skimmed through the document, and signed. "So let's hear it."

"Like I said, this is about geoengineering. We must prove that my methods of climate modification can produce a snowstorm in the middle of summer."

She laughed. "Is that some kind of stunt? What's the point?"

"Show the world something significant about global warming: that we don't have to be helpless victims."

Sam nodded. "I agree, but how will you—*we*—do that?"

"I've arranged to have a sulfur mixture added to the jet fuel on aircraft flying west from Seattle." He pointed a large map of western Washington State mounted to the wall above his desk.

Sam rolled her eyes. She knew where Seattle was located, but she didn't interrupt. Cooper loved showing off, so she humored him.

"The burning fuel disperses tons of sulfur dioxide particles into the atmosphere to mimic what happens after large volcanic eruptions. The particles block the sun's rays, thereby cooling Earth's surface."

"Right," she said. "The particles make a kind of shield called solar radiation management—SRM. But you're planning to implement it?"

"I already have."

"Seriously?" Sam pulled her chair closer to Cooper's desk and set down her lab notebook. "Every proposal I've read cautions that such an intervention should be tested on a small scale." She extended her right index finger. "First, it could disrupt air and water currents." She added her middle finger. "And second, it might cause floods and droughts."

"I'm targeting the Olympic Peninsula and Mount Olympus in particular, but yes, the cooling could affect the whole region."

Sam paused, analyzing his plan with her chemistry background in mind. "But doesn't that produce oxides of sulfur when burned? Won't those be harmful to the nickel-based alloys used in aircraft engines?"

Cooper grinned. "Good question, Sam. Normally, yes. But I've developed an additive to protect the surfaces inside the engines. Otherwise, they'd start to fail and the airlines would suspect something."

"You're doing this without authorization?" Sam frowned, and she felt a jolt of adrenaline. "Isn't that illegal? Why the secrecy? Why not get the airlines to try it openly? Seems like they would love to boast about being all eco-friendly."

"The clients who are providing the money want to keep the operation a secret."

Sam shook her head. "Doesn't that make you suspicious?"

"They want exclusive rights to my formula afterword, and they don't want anyone else to know about it."

Sam narrowed her eyes. Cooper was clever, but he couldn't ignore the laws of physics. "From what I've read, the sulfur dioxide has to be injected high into the stratosphere to create a sun shield, and commercial jets don't fly that high."

"That's a misconception," he said. "My modeling demonstrates that this will work if there are enough daily flights to East Asia to keep replenishing the shield." He stood and pointed to the curved lines of flight routes spreading out on the map from Seattle. "But we still need to demonstrate how well it actually works."

"Okay, but cooling a few degrees won't be enough to make it snow."

"That's only the first step. I've designed a fleet of boats equipped with powerful pumps." He opened a file drawer in his desk, pulled out a drawing, and showed it to her. "These boats spray seawater up into the marine cloud layer, which will increase their moisture content and cause them to reflect more sunlight. They will be unmanned drones that cruise in circles off the coast." Cooper tapped his index finger on a pattern of equally spaced dots on the map.

Sam knew Cooper was brilliant, but she had no idea he'd created such an elaborate scheme. She still couldn't see how it all would work. "So you'd be making the Olympic Mountains both wetter and colder."

"Correct again. But the clouds need an extra nudge to produce snow."

"Uh, how are you going to do that?"

"That technology is well established." Cooper folded his arms across his chest and leaned back in his chair, clearly pleased with himself. "You've heard of cloud seeding, right?"

"Sure, for rain but not snow."

"I've installed cloud seeding generators, basically propane burners, which spew silver iodide crystals into the clouds arriving off the Pacific. These crystals are seeds for converting droplets of supercooled water into snowflakes." Cooper started talking faster and waving his arms. "The *combined* effect of these three technologies will cause snowfall." He became so excited he stood up and began pacing, talking more to himself than to her.

She remained seated, watching him with a half smile—partly amused and partly annoyed at his self-absorption.

"People have only dreamed of controlling weather for years, and I've already designed the technology for doing it. Now the cartel is paying me a ton of money to realize my dream."

Sam gaped at Cooper. "*Cartel?*"

He stopped abruptly and turned to face her, his eyes wide with fear, realizing he'd said too much. He walked back to his desk and sat. "You'd find out eventually. The cartel consists of oil company executives I pitched to this weekend. They're the ones asking me to make it snow in July."

Sam contemplated what he'd just said for several seconds. "Why the hell do they care whether it snows in July?"

"Think about it, Sam. These men are in the business of selling oil and gas, which people believe are causing global warming—which they are, of course. There is more frequent talk about subsidizing renewables and implementing carbon taxes. If they can point to places that are cooling, it can sow doubt about how pervasive climate change really is."

"Your whole project is a scam, a fraud," she hissed. "There are reasons scientists don't take money from private funders. It's called 'ethics.'" She stood up, grabbed her notebook, and started to walk away.

"Don't be so quick to judge. Sit down and hear me out. You need the background."

Sam turned but remained standing. She had a hunch she knew what he was going to say because she'd already heard his sob story.

"Over the past five years, I've written a hundred proposals and made presentations to all the funding agencies." His voice strained. "They've *all* turned me down." His face turned red. "We're doing our research in a lab so cramped it hardly provides the space to move around the equipment. This project gives me the money I need to complete my life's work—the long-term solution to global warming."

Sam glared at him. "By giving this cartel what they want, countries will stay addicted to fossil fuels for years. Carbon dioxide will continue to increase, and what do we get? Hurricanes, wildfires, drought, floods. That's a pretty crappy life's work if you ask me."

"All those things are terrible, but . . ." Cooper got up and raised his hands, as if appealing to her. "That's why we'll be working like crazy to *reverse* the negative effects of fossil fuels. Your project is part of it. We'll be able to reduce atmospheric carbon dioxide within ten years or so—until it has returned to pre-industrial levels. Think about it. Our brains—*our* scientific minds—can engineer a cooler planet with temperatures that Thoreau or John Muir would recognize. But we need the money to prove it can be done."

Sam blinked. Cooper was going all evangelical on her, and she was struggling to maintain her skepticism. "So . . . so what exactly does this cartel want from you?"

Cooper smiled. "They want us to create heavy snow buildup on Mount Olympus, then blanket social media with evidence of the cold conditions. That's where I need your help in addition to your research skills. I want you to design and implement a social media campaign to alert people to the falling temperatures. To see the future of how we can end global warming."

Sam sank into her chair and shook her head. "I don't think this is a good—"

Cooper cut her off. "In return, I'll pay off your student debt and double your current stipend. But I'm not going to lie. This won't be easy. For seven months, starting this January, we'll be living in shelters high on Blue Glacier on Mount Olympus. Are you willing to do that?"

"You want me to go against everything I believe in as a scientist? That's asking an awful lot. The money is nice, but what about my career? I'd have to put aside my research for how long? A year or more?"

"Not a problem." Cooper's hands swished nonchalantly through the air. "I've told a colleague at MIT, Doris Hopper, about the innovative work you've done. She wants to talk to you about a post-doc position. Besides, you can keep working on it while we're on the mountain. Just bring the data you've already collected."

Cooper's eyes drilled into Sam's. "But listen to me. I know I'm asking a lot of you, Sam. Think about the amazing results you're getting with your research. Remember that's *my* formula you're testing. Together, you and I will be able to reverse climate change. Isn't that what matters most?"

"Yes. I want that more than anything." Sam met his gaze, feeling conviction to her core.

"Then look at what I'm asking of you as a brief, distasteful interlude followed by the biggest gift you can give humanity. I admit I've entered into a devil's bargain with the cartel. But I know what I'm doing. I can handle it."

Sam felt dizzy and a little nauseous. "This is a big change of direction in my life. I need time to think it over." It was as if Cooper were casting a spell over her, and she needed time to clear her head.

"You've got forty-eight hours. But know that I value your commitment, hard work, and intellect. If I didn't know you had the courage, I would have asked someone else. Opportunities like this come around only once in a lifetime. This will launch you into a career you've only dreamed about." He paused. "But I need to know in two days if you're with me on this. Two days."

———

Sam couldn't decide what to do about Cooper's proposal, and she often thought more clearly after intense exercise in the fresh air, so she suited up in a tank top and running tights to run a brisk five kilometers on the Caltech track. On lap three, she thought about being free of school debt and pulling in a pretty sweet salary, but by lap five she wondered if her job assignment would be too low level—more like something an undergraduate could do. On lap ten her cell phone rang in its pouch on her tights. She didn't recognize the number, and after answering, she didn't recognize the male voice either.

"You don't know me, Ms. Schroeder, but your boss, Dr. Cooper, works for my outfit. I understand he offered you a chance to ride along when he conducts his studies on Blue Glacier."

"Who is this? How did you know that?" The hair stood up on the back of Sam's neck and she felt like hanging up and running faster than ever. Cooper's proposal was disorienting enough without some stranger from the cartel contacting her on top of it.

"My name is Theodore Stone, but most people call me Tex."

Even before he gave his nickname, his drawl had told her he was from Texas.

"Never mind how I learned of your offer. I'd like to meet to make it more attractive. Not much time though. Can you join me at the Hollywood Burbank airport in thirty minutes?"

"Why don't you just tell me what you have in mind?"

"This kind of transaction is best done face-to-face. You'll want to hear what I have to say. It'll be worth your time."

She was having a hard time determining if this guy was for real, but if he wasn't, how would he even know about the deal with Cooper? "How can I find you once I get to the airport?"

"The gal at the General Aviation Desk will let me know when you're here. Don't be late. I'm outta here at three thirty."

"I'll be in my sweaty running clothes."

"No problem. Just be prompt."

While speeding from the track in Pasadena to the airport, Sam puzzled over how this guy could have known about her job offer. He said he was with the organization funding Cooper's geoengineering study, called the cartel. But this operation was supposed to be so confidential, Cooper had her sign a nondisclosure agreement. Now some stranger wanted to talk to her about it. Would this be a violation of the agreement she had just signed? She had more questions than answers, but she was intrigued to hear what he had to say. Maybe it could help her decide about Cooper's offer. If she could trust Cooper's instincts, it could change the course of her career.

The General Aviation Desk was near the back of a well-furnished waiting area with expensive couches, reflecting the kinds of jet-set customers it catered to. The people she saw milling about were clearly either business people or pilots, and she felt self-conscious in her tank top and running tights, but she was on time as Tex had insisted.

Soon a tall, slender man with a handlebar mustache appeared. His jeans, western shirt, and black Stetson identified him by themselves. His drawl clinched it. "Howdy. Thanks for showing up on time. Y'all come this way."

He seemed like a character in an old western movie. Sam followed the man out onto the hot asphalt tarmac. He strode so fast toward a parked private jet that she almost had to jog to keep up. There were no markings on the plane except for the tail number, but as she climbed the stairs and stepped inside, the circulating air was pleasantly cool and laced with the scent of leather. The jet was furnished like the living room of a tiny mansion with indirect lighting and plush furnishings. The opulence was intimidating, which was probably the reason Stone wanted to meet there.

"What's this all about?" Sam asked as he motioned for her to sit.

"Ms. Schroeder, can I call you Samantha?"

He sat across from her on a leather chair and propped his intricately tooled cowboy boots on the coffee table.

She shrugged. "Everybody calls me Sam."

"Well, Sam, what can I get you to drink? Beer? Wine? Margarita?"

"Perrier would be great." No way was she drinking alcohol.

Tex pressed a button and said, "Could you bring a Perrier and an Alamo Golden?" Then he turned back to her.

"I know that you agreed to not discuss Dr. Cooper's project. That was at our request, so it's not a violation of that agreement for us to talk openly about it now. We were so impressed with his geoengineering technology and his test protocol that we've made a substantial investment in it."

The whole encounter seemed surreal. Why had she rushed to meet a total stranger to talk about a major life decision she was grappling with? "Why did you want to talk with me?"

There was a knock, and a waiter emerged with his beer and her sparkling water. He set them on napkins on the coffee table.

"Thanks, Esteban," Tex said, and the waiter disappeared.

Tex sipped his beer. "We believe that Dr. Cooper is smart. But like many geniuses, he gets lost in his thoughts. You've worked with him for over a year, so I'm sure you've seen that too. Am I right?"

"He has his quirks. So what?" She folded her arms across her chest.

"We prefer our involvement with Dr. Cooper to be . . . anonymous. Even more important, there can be no leaks that the weather changes he is producing on Mount Olympus are man-made. It has to appear to be a place that is cooling naturally while the rest of the planet is heating up. We believe you can help ensure he doesn't slip and let people know what he's done."

"What are you asking me to do exactly?"

"I'm convinced you're the right gal for this. I want you to accept the position that Dr. Cooper has offered and accompany him to Blue Glacier. Once you're there, you'll send me weekly updates describing what you and he have accomplished. If you ever think he's compromising the operation's security, email me immediately. That's all you have to do. You'll warn us if he gets careless."

"Listen, I haven't decided if I even want to accept Cooper's offer. This whole thing might not be good for my career." She reached for the Perrier and sipped.

"Then you'd be missing out on a rare opportunity."

"Maybe. Maybe not. Spying on Cooper isn't very honest. Or ethical. Why should I agree to report to you behind his back?"

"Fair question. Dr. Cooper will pay you well, but I can offer you something additional. I understand that your mother has some medical issues and lives alone in San Jose. And she barely gets by on her Social Security. I'm willing to set up a trust in your name guaranteeing your mother's care for the rest of her life."

Sam's back straightened in alarm. "How do you know so much about me and my family?"

Tex held up his hand. "It wasn't hard to find out she receives government SSI benefits for her history of substance abuse and that her payments come through you. I feel for her. Ma had to take all us kids from Pa and raise us on her waitress salary because he was an abusive drunk. I'd feel good if you let us help your mom out. She will be well cared for, and you can take that to the bank. All you have to do is keep an eye on Dr. Cooper. You probably already do a heck of a lot of that anyway. He strikes me as a high-maintenance gent."

He gave Sam a calculated stare. "And the man can strut sitting down. You're going to have to put up with a lot of that for six or seven months. On a glacier. Without HBO." He grinned. "Why not get paid what you're really worth?"

"Cooper gave me until tomorrow to make up my mind. I'll let you know then." Sam stood to leave.

Tex shook his head, his casual smile replaced by a frown. "As they say in my home town, 'That dog don't hunt.'" His blue eyes locked on to hers, and he spoke emphatically in a deep voice. "When my plane leaves this airport, my offer is off the table. I need an answer *now*."

Sam froze. "You're saying all I have to do is write you a weekly status report and then tell you if I see Cooper getting careless?" Her own voice sounded weak to her, like it was coming from a little girl.

"That's it."

"I'll need something in writing before I leave this plane."

"I have a contract with the trust information already completed." Tex opened a briefcase and handed her a stack of paper.

"You knew I'd accept?"

"Let's just say we thought you might agree that we're giving you a lot for an itty-bitty investment of your time."

Sam skimmed the top two pages before looking up at Tex. "You'll pay Mom two thousand dollars a month? Then, if she needs institutional care, you'll cover the entire cost? We're talking tens of thousands of dollars."

"Just shows how important the success of this project is to our organization."

"When do the payments start?"

"As soon as you finish your assignment on Blue Glacier."

She hesitated while scanning the cabin and then dropped back down into her seat. "All right. I'll do it." Sam's shoulders fell as she sighed with relief, thinking about her mother being provided for the rest of her life. "Where do I sign?" Tex pointed to the line on the paper she was holding and handed her a pen.

Tex took the signed pages and handed her a gray box slightly larger than a cell phone. "One more thing. This here's a satellite modem, similar to a sat phone, only you don't talk into it. You attach it to your laptop and send us messages day or night, regardless of the weather or internet connection."

She studied the device in her hand. "I simply type messages on my laptop?"

"You bet. Anytime he isn't watching. But Dr. Cooper can't find out you're keeping an eye out for us. Is that clear?"

"Yes, sir, it is."

"Well, I guess that's all she wrote." They both stood and Tex shook Sam's hand.

On the drive back to Pasadena, Sam glanced at the little gray box on the seat next to her and thought about how she would tell Cooper she was accepting his offer. But then guilt hit her for spying on him and made her throat tighten up, overpowering the relief she had felt for arranging her mother's care. And the cost of this adventure to her career was yet to be seen. There were a lot of unknowns.-

6

The Flatiron Rock Formation
Boulder, Colorado

Wednesday, November 25

Grant sat precariously, catching his breath having climbed up from the base of the first of three Flatirons, a red rock formation jutting up from the mountainside southwest of Boulder. He looked down at the strangely small roofs of houses in the city spread out below him. Then he turned and followed the rope tied to the harness on his waist to Kate, who was scrambling up the rock face above him. He wondered what he'd been thinking when he agreed to the climb.

Grant had taken the job at NCAR, and in early November, he moved into a furnished cottage in the Chautauqua neighborhood up against the foothills on the west side of Boulder. His first goal was to understand the missions and projects of the various departments within the NCAR lab to identify solutions being developed to mitigate the climate crisis. This was part of his strategy of collecting positive stories to counter the numbing repetition of bleak climate news.

Kate flew to Boulder to join him for a visit during Thanksgiving week and offered to teach him a new adrenaline-filled way to unwind from a busy day like the surfing he had enjoyed when he worked in Santa Cruz.

"On belay," Kate called out as the rope pulled taught.

"Climbing." His shaky response felt more like a question than a statement as he planted his boots on the steeply sloping red rock. Kate had explained he should keep his weight out and away from the surface on those friction pitches without any handholds or footholds. He hoped he'd tied a firm knot where the rope attached to his climbing harness. Exposed, with nothing to grab, he felt his insides tighten and his legs go weak. Against Kate's instructions, his instinctual fear made him move closer to the rock, and his boots skidded and shot out from under him. Adrenaline and panic flooded his nervous system.

"Falling," he shouted as his weight stretched the rope. He bounced helplessly against the rock and the harness cut painfully into his thighs and waist.

"You're on belay, Grant. I've got you." Kate's strong voice was reassuring. "Scramble up any way you can. I'll take up the slack."

With the added security of the rope pulling him from above, Grant climbed, still trembling, past the ledge to the upper edge of the rock outcrop and joined Kate. From that point to the top, Grant found the climbing easier, with lots of places to hold on. He felt relief until he looked down the Flatiron's back side. They were on an overhang of a hundred feet above the forest floor below.

"We're going to rappel down from here," Kate said with a grin. "Another new adventure for you."

Grant swallowed hard and had begun to steel himself for dangling from the rope for a second time that morning when he heard a popping sound coming from the metal rod protruding from the top of the rock next to them. "What's that noise?" he shouted.

"Big problem," Kate said while coiling the rope. "That cloud above us is discharging static electricity to ground. No time to teach you to rappel because now lightning could strike any second."

The popping became a steady buzz, and Grant felt the hairs on his ears stand up as static electricity filled the air. He'd just experienced a life-threatening fall and now, minutes later, they both could be killed by lightning. Kate grabbed his hand and pulled them as far away from the metal rod as possible.

A flash of white light and simultaneous boom made them freeze as thunder echoed across the valley. Grant smelled ozone from the scorched air and realized lightning had struck close but missed them.

"Let's get down from here." Kate hurried back up to the top and draped their rope around the metal post and over the side, making sure it reached the ground at the base of the rock.

Grant followed Kate's instructions and was soon sliding slowly down the rope, bouncing while his boots pushed off the rock face as he went.

Kate joined him at the bottom. "Practice your friction pitches and you'll be a fine climber." She smiled. "You never let your fear stop you."

"Thanks, Kate." He smiled back at her. "You're a great teacher. I definitely wouldn't have attempted this with anyone else."

"Ha!" she replied. "This isn't the first time I've seen you take a risk physically. When we were on the glacier, you took risks without knowing what the outcome would be. You were right there with me. That's just one of the things I love about you." She leaned over and kissed his cheek.

They made their way back to Grant's car. "I want to show you around NCAR and my office," he said, "but first let's drive by one of the neighborhoods that burned in the late December wildfire near here." He drove slowly so she could take in the full effect of house after house burned down to the foundation with brick walls, chimneys, and scorched fences scattered where a peaceful neighborhood had once stood.

"It's creepy, Grant. Like driving past a dead body or something. How could this happen in an urban area like this?"

"I was told the winds were a hundred miles an hour. They turned the fire into a blowtorch."

"I've read that climate change played a role."

"The unusually wet spring produced tall grasses that were then turned to tinder during the dry fall with virtually no rain. It was unheard of to have such strong winds like they experienced at the end of December as a snow storm approached. All it took was a flame, and they're still trying to identify how that got started."

Kate released an audible sigh. "We'll probably be faced with more of this kind of disaster until we stop dumping greenhouse gases into the atmosphere. It's really disheartening. I guess there's no place in the world to escape climate change."

At NCAR Grant and Kate walked past the displays of extreme weather phenomena and the instruments used to study them. Other displays indicated the increase in greenhouse gases and the corresponding impact on climate. Grant took Kate's hand and guided her to a hallway off the main lobby where a sign reading "Promising Solutions" referred to displays yet to be hung.

"Grant, is this your doing?" Kate asked with a smile.

"Yep. This whole wall will be populated with photos and descriptions of projects from around the world that can slow and eventually reverse the warming."

"I'm impressed. You're already making a difference."

"Come with me. I'll introduce you to someone who's doing some important research."

Grant found Dr. Liu Yang in her office and introduced Kate. "Dr. Yang analyzes mathematical models of a form of geoengineering to study how aerosols might be injected into the stratosphere to cool the planet. She and I formed an informal science advocacy group of scientists here, and she co-facilitates it."

"Grant has a way of bringing out the hidden talent in our colleagues," Liu said. "In the short time he's been here, he's managed to change these shy introverts into strong advocates in the community for fighting climate change. We're really glad to have him at NCAR."

Kate turned and smiled at Grant. "He was key to my research on Blue Glacier last summer too."

A little later, Kate stood in front of the floor-to-ceiling window in Grant's office admiring the view, from the foothills of the Rocky Mountains to the prairie and all the way to the eastern horizon. Grant joined Kate and put his arm around her waist. "The climate scientists in this building are the best in the world, but even they can't convince some people to take the climate crisis seriously. My goal now is to help people know that things are being done to solve global warming. We can't afford to abandon hope."

"Thank God the committee voted to let my station stand. I've started interviewing and recruiting students for next summer's research on the glacier. Soon we'll see if our efforts make the difference we hope."

7

Blue Glacier
Olympic National Park

Tuesday, June 7

The helicopter rose up the flanks of Mount Olympus's forested peaks toward its destination: Blue Glacier. A charter pilot was flying Kate to the research station to check it out before the new batch of students joined her later in the week. As the snow-covered glacier came into view, it was like coming home to her favorite spot on the planet. She looked forward to a few days of solitude in this familiar wilderness. After an exhausting school year—and so much department politics—this time alone to prepare the station for her students seemed more like a retreat to recharge her soul.

Through the canopy, she could make out patches of scattered fog that were all that remained of the dense overcast blanketing the Olympic Peninsula for the past several days. She stared, mesmerized, at the blur of trees and dense undergrowth passing below. The hypnotic drumbeat of the rotors was reduced to dull whumps in her noise-canceling headset, and she began to drift off.

"We've got ice." The voice of Jack, the pilot, boomed through the intercom.

Her head snapped from the wisps of fog surrounding them to the frost he pointed to forming on the canopy. Looking down, she saw a thick crust of white rime ice collecting on the metal skid of the helicopter. A moment later the pitch of the engine dropped and Kate stared, horrified, at the tops of trees she was sure were going to crash through the plexiglass bubble.

"What's happening? Why are we dropping?" she asked, her chest tightening.

"Ice buildup," Jack grunted as he fought the stick to level the chopper. Kate felt the pinch of the belt across her lap as her seat dropped out from under her.

"This is bad," he yelled. "Can't keep her up."

Kate grabbed her seat with both hands and braced for the impact she expected any second. "I don't like this," she yelled. "Can't we go back to the airport?"

"No way." Jack spoke with resolute urgency, his tone even and determined. "Got to land or we'll crash."

She looked down at the rugged terrain of Glacier Meadows coming up toward them. They were so close she could make out the firepits in the campground and the trail leading down the mountain. Nothing looked remotely clear enough for them to set down without scattering parts of the helicopter, and probably themselves, through the trees.

"I'll try for the glacier," Jack said, looking up at the band of white above them.

Kate followed his gaze and glimpsed Panic Peak towering overhead. We'll never make it, she thought.

The engine whined as Jack forced power to the rotors, which tore into the air, clawing for lift. The helicopter hovered, barely above the treetops. The engine shook the frame of her seat, and the air grew thick with the acrid blend of fuel and exhaust fumes. It was a contest—gravity's pull on the heavy, thick ice versus the lift from the rotor blades frantically beating the air. She sensed that every rivet and bolt of the helicopter was straining to keep them aloft. She'd had many close calls during her years of research on this remote glacier, but this seemed hopeless. Adrenaline surged through her and her hands shook.

As the pilot cautiously tugged the control stick, they stopped sinking. Through bands of fog, Kate could make out the tip of the glacier above them with its patchwork of blue ice, white snow, and layers of black rock debris. They floated over the cascading water of Glacier Creek, which gushed out between the ice and smooth rock below so loud she could hear it in spite of her headset and over the whine of the straining engine.

Kate had visions of dropping into that ice-cold stream as Jack applied firm but gentle nudges to the controls. The helicopter struggled a few feet higher, and she pictured them landing on the steeply sloping ice only to slide backward into the river.

She held her breath, urging the machine to climb higher through her sheer force of will. It inched up slowly to where Kate could just make out the surface of the ice above them. They struggled up over the lip to a spot that was flat but scored with deep crevasses. Although a smooth spot lay a hundred yards further up, the engine had no more to give.

"This'll have to do," Jack said.

Kate felt the hard jolt in her chest and heard a crunch of metal as they hit the ice, the skids spanning a crevasse with its blue opening directly below them.

Jack looked from side to side. "We're not slipping, are we?"

"No," she replied, "but I think we landed on some kind of metal frame. I can see it under us. We're in a precarious spot."

"Can't be helped." He shut off the engine.

After a pause, they both giggled nervously and whooped in relief.

"We'd better hold still," Jack warned. "Our shifting weight could tip us into the crevasse. You can take off your headset though." Kate set her bulky earpieces in her lap as Jack flipped switches on the control panel in front of him.

"What just happened?" Kate asked.

He sat back stiffly with his eyes closed, arms dangling at his side. After a minute he said, "Whew! That was intense."

"What *happened*?" Kate repeated, more insistently.

He turned to face her, looking somber. "Icing. On fixed-wing planes it breaks up airflow and lift. It's the same on helicopters because it disrupts efficient airflow over the rotor blades. And it adds a ton of weight."

"How could we ice up now?" she asked. "It's June."

"Could happen anytime there's humidity like fog and freezing temps."

Kate looked around at the snow surrounding them. "How cold is it?"

Jack glanced down at a thermometer attached to the canopy. "Outside it's just a degree below freezing, but the air above could be colder."

"You made a good call, flying up to the glacier." She sighed. "I wasn't sure we'd make it."

"Me either, but we had a little reserve power. If the carburetor had iced up completely, we'd have been toast."

"What do we do now? Seems like we're stuck."

"Sit tight. The fog's burning off, and the full sun will reach us soon. It'll melt the ice. I think I can still get you to the research station this morning."

As they waited for the line of direct sunlight to reach where they sat in the shadow of the peaks to the east, Kate studied the scene around them. "I hardly recognize this place. Look at the drifts. That tells me the snow is fresh powder. The flakes haven't had time to melt."

"We've got company." Jack pointed toward two dark figures wearing parkas approaching his side of the helicopter walking stiffly on snowshoes. The figures, one a head taller than the other, stopped a few feet in front of the canopy. She and Jack stared in silence as the standoff continued.

"This is weird," Kate finally said. "What do you think they want?"

The taller of the two pulled back the hood of his parka, revealing blond, curly hair and a face with a strong chin. He cupped both hands over his ears like he was putting on headphones and held up a small black box with an antenna on top.

"He wants to talk to us on the radio," Jack said as he replaced his headset and flipped a switch on the control panel. "He'll assume we're still on the Port Angeles airport frequency."

Kate replaced her headset too.

Jack pressed the talk button on the control stick. "You guys on Port Angeles?"

"You guessed right," came a deep voice, loud and crisp. "It's against the law to land here. It's restricted national park airspace."

"I'm Dr. Landry," Kate said. "I'm head of the University of Washington's Atmospheric Sciences Blue Glacier Project. We're headed to our station near Snow Dome. We have a waiver from the Park Service to fly there."

"Maybe so," the voice on the radio said, "but you're a long way from the station."

"Who am I talking to?" Kate demanded.

"I'm Dr. Mark Cooper, head of the Caltech Glacier Ablation Project. Dr. Landry, your helicopter just crushed one of our remote weather stations."

"Sorry, Dr. Cooper. It was either land or crash. Our copter iced up."

"Your pilot should check the weather during his preflight. We'll send you a bill for the damage. Out." Both figures turned and began climbing back up the glacier.

"He's full of shit!" Jack said over the intercom. "I always check the weather, but the glacier has its own microclimate. There's no one here to report it."

"I know. I watched you plan. Since when has Caltech shown any interest in Blue Glacier? They've not had a team here since the 1970s. Now this guy acts like he owns the place. Jack, when we take off, let's fly over the old Caltech site and see if we can tell what's going on."

An hour later when the full sun reached the helicopter, Kate watched the frost on the canopy turn to droplets. Water glistened on the thin coating of ice that remained on the skids. "It's melting fast."

"It's now or never." Jack threw some switches and the engine whined, then roared to life. After letting it idle, he engaged the rotor, and they lifted gently off the ice. Kate breathed a sigh of relief to be on their way again, but the close call they'd just had was too fresh. Would they be able to climb another thousand feet without icing up again?

As the helicopter lifted off, Kate's fear was replaced by amazement at all the new snow she saw through the canopy. Her friend, Ranger Ben, had been right. There was a ton more snow this year. Where there had always been dark rock outcrops, she saw nothing but white. Never before had she seen the retreating terminus covered in so much fresh snow. It was exciting to think Blue Glacier might actually be growing.

Further up the glacier, along the base of Snow Dome, she could make out three white structures with curved tops, modern versions of the Quonset huts common in World War II, each covered with a layer of snow. They'd been there a while. Since they were located on what had been the Caltech camp in the past, Kate assumed these shelters were Cooper's base of operation.

As the helicopter circled the campsite, she saw that the snow around the structures had been trampled, but there was no sign of life. Three vertical antennas and what appeared to be a satellite dish were mounted beside one of the shelters, along with a white box on stilts, probably an enclosure for weather instruments. A few feet away stood an anemometer mounted at the top of a pole with its cups spinning steadily—evidence of a breeze.

"This appears to be a normal field research operation," Kate said to Jack. "Maybe heavier on radio communications than typical for glacial research. I've seen enough. Let's get up to Snow Dome and check out our station."

Still nervous after their close call getting to the glacier, she wondered if they could climb yet another thousand feet. Her concern evaporated when the helicopter rose steadily straight up alongside the steep snow-covered slope.

"Let's circle the station before we land." Kate pointed to the saddle to the northwest of Snow Dome. Looking down at UW's station anchored to the rocks, she could see that a massive snow-drift had formed against the west wall up to the roofline, and she could barely make out a small portion of the generator shed near the top of another huge drift. "The station's almost buried. What the heck is going on?"

Jack had no response.

When they circled back to the landing spot on top of Snow Dome and hovered, the rotor kicked up so much loose snow, they were engulfed in a small blizzard. Normally, by June, the snow would have melted and compressed into the sugary texture of firn, a transitional form between snowflakes and solid ice. This snow was fresh, probably from the storm the week before.

Jack shut off the engine. "Good thing you brought snowshoes. You'll need them."

Kate said goodbye, strapped on her snowshoes, and began walking unsteadily toward the station. Even with proper equipment, she struggled, and the snow found its way into her boots and up her pant leg. Had she landed on an alien planet? The general contours were familiar, but only Panic Peak, rising up beyond the station, remained a recognizable landmark. The helicopter took off, and she waved to Jack as he flew directly overhead.

The quarter-mile hike took forever, and Kate dragged her duffel over the snow rather than carry it on her shoulder. When she reached the station, she navigated around the drifts up to the door, which luckily was not blocked by snow. After dropping her gear in the entry room, she used a shovel stored there to clear a path from the entrance to the small generator shed that also served as a privy. The path cut through deep snowdrifts in spots, but in other places it went across bare rock that had been cleared of snow by the wind.

She finally reached the shed and tried to start the engine powering the generator, but although the battery turned the big flywheel, the diesel wouldn't fire. Without the generator she and her students could only last a day or two on battery power for their laptops, communications radio, and lights. She started talking to herself. "Stop draining the battery and think. The air temperature is colder than normal. Because it's a diesel, the fuel oil gets thick when it's this cold. Try warming it up."

She returned to the station and grabbed a blowtorch and an assortment of wrenches and screwdrivers. Back at the generator, she ran the flame up and down the length of the copper fuel line from the tank to the engine. After five minutes, she cranked the engine again. It chugged to life, blue smoke spewing from the exhaust.

She let it warm up while she dug out the window on the west side of the station where snow had drifted to the roof. Since she only needed power for the lights after dark and her computer, she stopped the generator and stood on the path, relishing the quiet and scanning her surroundings.

After studying the drifts on the steep slopes around the station, she knew her team of students would need to be careful to avoid starting avalanches. If only Ed LaChapelle were there. Although he'd been dead for years, he had once been the country's leading expert on avalanche surveillance and avoidance. Ed had built the Blue Glacier Project station and established the UW position that Kate now held. A tattered copy of his classic reference book, *Field Guide to Snow Crystals*, was still on the shelf above the desk at the station. She'd use it to analyze the snowflakes for their potential avalanche threat. Someday that old book might even save their lives.

Kate went inside and used a rag to wipe off the layer of dust that coated everything, as it did each winter, and put away the food and supplies she'd brought for the week. Sunlight reflecting off the brilliant white snow streamed through the windows, and Kate felt comfortable now that the oil heater had removed the chill.

She loved gazing at the familiar books, wall posters, and dishes, brought up over the decades by various scientists, faculty, and students from the university while they collected data. The simple, rustic accommodations reminded her of the modest ranch house in western Wyoming where she had grown up. She felt at home up here.

Among the familiar objects, she saw one that had been invented by one of the previous year's students, Charlie. The spark-gap device in a mason jar he'd created responded to the static electricity during thunderstorms. If only the plane taking him and another student to the hospital hadn't been forced down, they both might still be alive. Remembering last year's crisis made Kate's stomach tighten. Charlie's lips had turned blue and he'd needed oxygen to survive. At the time, no one knew that the mammoth buried in the ice contained a deadly virus or that Charlie had breathed it in. Alice contracted the same illness soon after. What an awful irony that Tom's single-engined ski plane lost a ski on takeoff and was forced to land on a sandbar next to the Hoh River. They were all found dead from the awful disease.

This got Kate thinking about Grant and how helpful he'd been to her then. He could have run away. Instead, he'd hiked to join her at the research station to support her excavation of the mammoth under strict preventive healthcare protocols. How she missed having him with her now. She'd just have to let it go and focus on what she could accomplish.

After lunch she reviewed her research plans for the summer in light of the conditions she'd encountered that morning. Travel with snowshoes would be slow and hazardous. Unlike previous summers, this year, avalanches were a greater threat than falling into crevasses. Still, the team would need to travel the glacier to install weather instruments. They would also need to determine the depth and density of snow and ice in several places to document how much the glacier might be growing. For sure, with the cold temperatures and significant snowfall, the glacier's mass balance would have increased.

Now, for the first time, she could study, describe, and document a rare event: a mountain glacier that was growing. She realized this might be a short-lived anomaly, but still, what a once-in-a-lifetime opportunity.

After cooking dinner on the propane stove, she washed the dishes using water from melted snow heated on the stove. This mundane routine was part of what made her stay alone at the station so relaxing. Then she grabbed her parka, put on her boots, and went outside to gaze at the sky, marveling at clouds that looked like they were on fire with the oranges and reds of the setting sun.

She stood in the cold, still air hoping to see the "green flash" as the sun dropped below the sharp line of the Pacific—that rare trick of nature she had witnessed with Grant the summer before when the last rays of the sun's spectrum momentarily flashed green. No such luck, and as it began to get dark, she started the generator. When she went back inside, she felt something she had never noticed before, a distinct vibration through the floorboards from the rhythmic chugging of the motor in the shed mounted to the rocks. The heavy flywheel must have gotten out of balance somehow.

As she sat writing by the light of the bare bulb over the table, becoming absorbed in her work, she heard a scraping sound outside on the rocks, followed a moment later by banging on the door. Her heart nearly stopped. Who could that possibly be? Alone on the mountain, she felt vulnerable, and springing up, she knocked over her mug of tea.

Her only possible weapon was her ice ax, which she grabbed as she rushed to the entry, and shouted, "Who's there?"

The reply was immediate. "Dr. Cooper and Sam, your neighbors."

Neighbors? As far as she knew, she had no neighbors. "Hold on," she called out. After pausing a moment to gather herself, she opened the door a crack but could barely make out two figures wearing headlamps that glared in her eyes. They appeared to be the pair who'd confronted her and Jack in the helicopter that morning.

The tall one pointed toward the ax in her hand. "Expecting trouble?"

"Well, I sure didn't expect visitors." She hesitated, blinded by the headlamp. "What do you want?"

"We heard the motor and decided to investigate." The speaker turned off his headlamp. It was Cooper. "I guess you made it here after crushing our weather station. This is my research assistant, Sam."

A woman pulled off her hood, and long red hair flowed down her back. "Hi, I'm Samantha Schroeder," she said, reaching out to shake Kate's hand.

Kate shook hands and smiled, realizing she had assumed Sam was a man, and she opened the door wider. "You can come in. Leave your coats and boots here in the entry." She pointed to hooks on the wall behind her next to the coiled climbing ropes.

They left their snowshoes and ski poles outside and kicked off the loose snow from their boots before entering.

"Have a seat," Kate said, motioning to the bench across the table from where she had been working as she started the burner under a pot on the stove. "I'll make some tea."

While waiting for the water to boil, she sized up her visitors. Cooper was in his early forties, tall and fit with curly blond hair. Sam was an attractive woman she guessed in her upper twenties, sitting quietly, but attentive to what Cooper was saying. Kate was curious about what brought them to the glacier. "What do you think of all this snow?"

"It's exciting. That's why we're here—to document this stuff," Cooper replied.

"You just set up camp?"

"No. We came up in January. I assumed the heavy rains they were having would mean more snow in the mountains, so I'm here to monitor the buildup."

Kate brought two mugs with tea bags and spoons from the sink counter and set them on the table.

"I read about you after learning that you do field work on Blue Glacier," he added.

Kate sat down on the bench across from the pair. "I don't suppose you found it interesting."

"Oh, but I did," Cooper said. "There's a lot online about your mammoth."

Kate was eager to change the subject. "You camped out all winter in this?"

"Yes. We rode out some wild storms and collected some amazing data. Right, Sam?"

She nodded. "Yeah. The wind speeds were incredible. Gusts over a hundred and snow falling faster than—"

"We've recorded every storm since January," Cooper said, cutting her off.

Sam's eyes narrowed and she glared at Cooper but remained quiet.

Still hoping to learn what brought the two to the glacier, Kate asked, "What are you trying to show with your research? Why is Caltech interested?"

"As I'm sure you know, Caltech scientists used to study this glacier years ago but shifted focus to Greenland and the Arctic," Cooper replied. "But now with the snow buildup, we're documenting the changes with external funding and Caltech's authority. How about you?"

"UW never left Blue Glacier, and I've led a team of graduate students each summer for the past nine years."

"I read about the problems you had last summer. All those deaths. Must have been tough."

"It was bad, but we're back. A team will be joining me in a few days."

Cooper frowned and looked at Sam but didn't comment.

Kate continued. "My past research documented a glacier in retreat. But this year we have a unique opportunity. Like you, we'll start monitoring the weather and try to understand what caused it to change so abruptly."

"I wouldn't bother if I were you," Cooper said, gesturing with the back of his hand as if he were brushing away a fly.

Kate's back stiffened. "What do you mean? *You're* here."

"That's my point. We've been collecting data for months. What else could you add?"

Kate didn't have a good answer. "We'll have to see. My team and I will be working on it."

"Come down to our camp and I'll show you our setup. Maybe then you'll see how I've covered all the bases."

"That will have to wait 'til after my students arrive." She couldn't take any more of Cooper's attitude of superiority. Nor was she fooled by his attempt to preempt her research. She'd never participated in university rivalry, but Cooper apparently wanted a win for Caltech.

"At least take this." He held out a small, handheld radio transceiver.

"What's that for?" Kate asked.

"You're alone on the mountain. We can use these radios to communicate if there's an emergency. Consider it a welcome gift."

"Okay. Thanks. I hope neither of us has to use it." Kate took the transceiver and set it on the desk.

After Cooper and Sam left, Kate sat with a cup of tea, thinking. His attempt to discourage her and her team from studying the weather seemed unnecessarily competitive. Having more data and scientific perspectives was always helpful. He seemed to be particularly curious about her plans. Why would Caltech initiate a research project on the glacier here after so many years? What was so urgent to justify spending what must have been a hellish winter on the mountain? Something just didn't add up.

8

University of Washington Research Station
Blue Glacier

Wednesday, June 8

Kate woke promptly at five and sprang out of her bunk to get a start on the busy day she'd planned. The sun was already highlighting the silhouettes of the peaks to the east and would soon shine on the research station itself. After a quick breakfast, she began recording the weather conditions in her journal: Clear skies. Air temperature minus 2 degrees C. Humidity: 45%. These were all within the range she would normally see except for the temperature, which was a good twenty degrees Celsius below normal.

Kate was curious about the wind, which could indicate how frequent and intense the storms had been that winter. She climbed the tower next to the station with the anemometer on top and read the dial. Each morning her team of student researchers would record the amount of wind passing the station. It had been nearly a year since the last reading due to the student illnesses and the massive storm that caused the station's abandonment. In addition to the fear of contracting the illness affecting the students, a major storm had threatened to destroy the building itself. Kate and Grant had hiked to safety.

The anemometer read fifteen thousand miles, which translated into about fifty miles per day—a huge increase in the volume of wind. She didn't need the anemometer to tell her there'd been a lot of wind because that was obvious from the volume of snow in drifts around the station. She took photographs from every angle and then used a ten-foot pole to measure and record the depth of the drifts within fifty feet of the station.

That afternoon, Kate examined samples of the powder snow under the powerful microscope she had previously used for studying pollen samples and recorded the snowflake images using the digital camera attached to the microscope. Comparing her images to the photographs in LaChapell's *Field Guide to Snow Crystals*, she could tell the snow around the station had fallen less than a week before. The flakes showed little melting and consolidation into coarse grains. Her team would be confronted with weather and snow conditions that could easily take them all summer to explain. Kate found the scientific challenge an exciting puzzle to be solved, and she looked forward to setting her new crop of students loose to solve it.

As the sun dropped below the line of the Pacific Ocean on the horizon west of the station, Kate started the generator and felt the vibration from the motor just as she had the day before, but this time, the tremors felt stronger, traveling through the rocks to her boots. She'd have to check the flywheel first thing the next morning.

9

Caltech Research Site
Blue Glacier

Wednesday, June 8

Sitting at his desk in the operations shelter, Cooper had watched anxiously through the shelter door window for daylight to turn to dusk. Finally, he heard the sound he was waiting for, the faint, rhythmic thumping of the diesel generator motor a mile away at the UW research station. He sucked in a breath, pressed his lips into a tight line, and waited ten seconds—long enough he thought for Landry to get safely back inside. It was time. He glanced over at Sam, who was bent over her laptop, compiling the summary data for the day. She wasn't paying any attention to him.

His hand shook as it hovered over the button on a remote detonator, but he *had* to do it. This was the only way he could think of to get Landry off Blue Glacier. If she and her students studied the unusual weather as planned, they could expose his plot, dooming his solution for global warming, his life's work, and worse still, causing the cartel to make him pay the price they threatened. He couldn't risk letting that happen. He pressed the button, sending a radio signal to a receiver to detonate an explosive charge he had secretly installed earlier that afternoon on the side of Panic Peak using one of his drones.

A penetrating roar vibrated their shelter. God, it sounded like a train careening off the track and crashing into the mountain.

Sam's head popped up, her eyes wide. "What the *hell?*"

"Avalanche!" he called, and his voice cracked. He was surprised at how constricted his throat was. The avalanche sounded deadly, and even though he'd triggered this catastrophe, he felt real fear creeping up his spine.

"*Shit!*" Sam replied as she came halfway out of her chair, ready to run.

"Stay calm. It's a ways off, I think." He wasn't sure whether he was trying to reassure Sam or himself. She'd been jumpy lately.

"This is so *not* what I signed up for," she said.

"It's fine! Relax." He knew Landry might be buried under fifteen feet of snow if she'd been caught outside in the avalanche, but he hoped she'd made it to safety and would just get the hell off the mountain. If not, well, it was regrettable, but he had no choice. He had to do what was necessary to protect his work and ensure the secrecy of his operation.

A few minutes passed. Cooper watched as Sam stormed to their makeshift kitchen at the far end of the shelter, poured whiskey into a plastic cup, downed it in one gulp, and glared at him.

Suddenly he remembered the radio transceiver on his desk. If Landry was still alive, she might call him for help. This was her disaster to survive—or not—and he wasn't about to rush to her rescue. As soon as Sam moved to return the whiskey bottle to the cabinet, he flipped off the transceiver switch and swiveled back to his computer. His work for the day was done, but he stared at the graphs on the screen without absorbing the meaning they were designed to convey.

He heard Sam plop down in her chair and slap her palms on her desk. "Well? Aren't you going to call Dr. Landry to see if she's okay?"

Cooper froze. It took him a second, but he spoke to Sam over his shoulder, trying to make his voice sound even. "Sorry. I almost forgot she's up here too. Why don't *you* hail her on our handheld? The avalanche sounded like it was in the other direction, but better safe than sorry." He was afraid to watch as Sam picked it up, but when she tried to call, they heard nothing but static.

10

University of Washington Research Station
Blue Glacier

Wednesday, June 8 and Thursday, June 9

Part way back to the station door, Kate heard a muffled "whumpf" from above the station, high on the side of Panic Peak, followed by a rumble that turned to a roar. The approaching wall of snow thundered down the mountain. Sprinting the last few yards just as the cloud hit the far end of the station, she slammed the outer door behind her and dove under the table. The entire building bucked. The steel cables crisscrossing the roof groaned, and it felt like an earthquake. Books and dishes crashed on all sides, bouncing off the shelves and onto the floor. Glass shattered as snow blasted the windows inward, followed by the gut-wrenching groan of boards splintering. The lights flickered and went out. Then silence.

It took a few minutes for Kate's adrenaline to settle down enough for her to assess her situation as she knelt, head down. Reaching out in total darkness, she felt the table above her, still standing, apparently. Nothing hurt and she didn't seem to have any injuries.-

As she began crawling across the floor, she felt the cold grains of snow, and something sharp cut into her palm. She imagined shards of dishes and window glass scattered across the floor. She'd have to crawl carefully. Where was the flashlight? Hadn't she seen it on the desk? She came to the bench, knocked over on its side.

What was that rotten egg smell? Propane gas. The line to the stove must have ruptured, and the flame from the oil heater could ignite it and blow up the station! When she first arrived, she had opened the shutoff valve under the kitchen sink, where the gas line came in. She found the cupboard door, ripped it open, and felt blindly for the valve. Her fingers, wet from sweat and probably blood from her cut palm, kept slipping. It took crawling halfway into the cupboard to get enough leverage to close the valve.

After groping around a few more minutes, she found the flashlight where it had rolled off the desk and come to rest against the oil heater. When she turned it on and scanned the room, Kate could hardly breathe. The damage took her breath away. Snow covered the floor below the broken windows, and the rest of the floor was a jumble of dinnerware, glass, and books that had fallen off shelves. The back wall had been forced inward at the roofline with snow and debris spilling onto the top bunks. She marveled that she'd survived and was thankful the students weren't there.

When Kate tried to open the door to the outside, it wouldn't budge. It had to be blocked by snow. Feeling trapped and helpless, the anxious feeling of adrenaline rush set in again. She thought about Dr. Cooper and wondered if he might be able to help. Frantically, she scanned the rubble on the floor with the flashlight beam and finally spotted the radio buried underneath a pile of books that had fallen off the shelf.

When she finally reached it, crawling through the rubble, she turned it on, pressed the transmit button, and spoke into the speaker. "Hello, Caltech camp. This is the UW research station." There was nothing but static. She tried twice more with the same result. Her signal was probably blocked by all the snow the avalanche had piled on top of the station.

She doubted his camp was in the path of an avalanche from Panic Peak, but maybe he'd heard the avalanche and would come to investigate. Another avalanche was unlikely, and it would be a lot easier to evaluate her situation in daylight. After sweeping glass and snow to the sides of the room with a broom, she sat exhausted on the bench next to the table, waiting for morning. She kept thinking how she was trapped and could die there before anyone realized she was missing.

———

The glowing numbers on Kate's watch told her it was after daybreak, but she saw no light coming through the windows—just a deep blackness like she had experienced only once before when exploring a cave. Her flashlight revealed her breath coming in clouds in the freezing air, so she put on her parka but dared not start a fire with all the openings blocked. Despite throwing her full weight against the door, it wouldn't budge. She felt the bitter taste of panic rising in her chest. Even if someone were to check on her, it might not be possible to reach the door, let alone open it, with the tons of snow and debris that had probably buried the station.

What about the windows? Maybe she could dig her way out. Using the snow shovel kept near the entry, she broke out the remaining glass from the opening nearest the bunks and started scooping snow onto the floor. She dug frantically out and up, wondering how deep the snow could be and thinking she would surely break through it at some point.

The snow was so compacted she was able to carve niches for her hands and feet. Pressing with her back against the wall for support was like scaling a rock chimney in her rock-climbing experience. Then she saw a hint of light filtering through the snow above and finally the glorious blue sky. Sucking in a deep breath of fresh air, she thought this must be how trapped miners felt at the moment of rescue.

The scene outside looked far worse than inside. The avalanche had brought tons of snow and rock debris, completely surrounding and burying the station. Thankfully, the steel cables that anchored the building to the rocks had held. But all that remained of the generator shed was a trail of half buried broken and splintered boards, scattered down the slope below the rock outcrop it was built on. Ironically, the toilet seat of the privy remained upright, but the diesel-powered generator lay on its side, still attached to its heavy wooden mounting beams. The flywheel, which lay partially buried, had been pulled off with enough force to bend the crankshaft.

After seeing the destruction, Kate was shaken but thankful to be alive. If she hadn't made it back into the station when she did, she'd be lying dead underneath the pile of snow and debris. The massive drifts on the side of Panic Peak must have created conditions ripe for breaking loose. She wondered if something as minor as the generator's vibration through the rocks could have triggered an avalanche and wished she'd checked on the flywheel when she'd first noticed it.

She couldn't imagine how the station could be restored in time for that summer's research. Kate considered herself strong and a survivor, but it seemed she wasn't meant to return to Blue Glacier. She nearly crashed on the helicopter ride to the station. Then the station was hit by an avalanche. She began to question whether her research and teaching were worth the risks of coming back, but she was determined to find a way, somehow, to bring students here to learn about glaciers and experience its pristine beauty before the ice melted away for good. She just had to find a way to do it safely.

She crawled down through the tunnel to the window, went back inside, and retrieved the transceiver Cooper had given her, thinking she might have success in the open air. Standing on the mound of snow coving the station, she gave it a try. "Caltech camp, UW research station here."

"Receiving you loud and clear," Sam replied.

Kate was so relieved to hear another person, her voice broke with emotion. "Thank God! I nearly died in an avalanche."

"Are you okay? We heard the roar and worried about you."

"Just a little scratched up, but the station is damaged and completely buried."

"I'm so sorry to hear that. What help do you need?"

"Could you contact the Port Angeles airport for me and have them send my charter pilot, Jack Thompson, to pick me up?"

"Will do. Hold on a minute."

After a pause, Sam came back on. "Your pilot will head your way soon. Meanwhile, Cooper and I plan to climb up there to help. Are you out of danger from more avalanches?"

"I think so. It looks like the loose snow above me has all come down. Having your company would be great. I'm pretty shaken up."

"We'll see you in a bit. Out."

Back inside the station, Kate swept the beam of her flashlight around the room. The broken glass and dishes, along with the books, could be cleared off the floor fairly quickly. Repairing the north wall where the boards had been forced inward, allowing snow to spill onto the upper bunks, would require a lot more work. She wondered if she and her students could make the repairs and dig out the door to regain access to the station in time to salvage the summer research season. She didn't know how, but she would try.

Kate stuffed the clothes she would need, along with her laptop and research notes, into a canvas duffel bag and took one final look at the old topo maps on the walls and the table where she and her students had shared meals and discussed research over the years. Would this be the end of her career on Blue Glacier? The thought of leaving for good was almost unbearable.

When Cooper approached the station, Kate was sitting on one of the broken boards where the generator shed had once stood, her duffel bag on the board next to her. Splintered and scattered shed boards and a lumpy pile of rough snow, ice, and rock were all that remained of the UW research station.

"Your helicopter pilot is on his way," he called out from a few yards away.

Kate stood. "Thanks for contacting him for me."

"What a mess," Sam said as she caught up with Cooper.

"I'm afraid so. This is the second time in two years I've had to leave here early. I really appreciate your coming up here."

"It's a shame about your research," Cooper lied. "But we'll see you get our reports on the weather."

All three looked up at the sound of the approaching helicopter. "We'll go with you to meet the pilot," Sam said.

Kate bent down to strap on her snowshoes. "Thanks. I hope to be back before the end of the summer."

Cooper looked around at the wreckage. "Doesn't look likely." He struggled to maintain a somber demeanor while inside he felt nothing but relief.

He and Sam climbed up Snow Dome with Kate to the waiting helicopter, and Kate introduced them to Jack. Cooper could tell from Jack's curt hello that he was still annoyed at his earlier comment about Jack's not checking the weather.

After the helicopter took off and they waved goodbye, Cooper and Sam returned to the site of the research station.

Cooper stood on the boards from the shed. "Take a look at this, Sam." He leaned down and hoisted the heavy flywheel, lying half buried, up onto its edge. "Now's a good time for you to take the pictures we talked about."

"Well, okay, but it's not a pretty scene." She unpacked her camera and photographed what remained of the research station from every possible angle.

"Be sure to shoot video too."

"I know, I know."

Cooper could hear the annoyance in her voice, but he let it go. While Sam was focused elsewhere, he removed the weights he had fastened to the flywheel, making it unbalanced so it would seem to Kate Landry that the avalanche was an accident.

"When we get back," Cooper called, "get those pictures uploaded and transmitted back to the cartel on the encoded satellite phone."

"Will do, boss," Sam replied curtly.

She seemed testy lately. Six months alone on a remote glacier was tougher than he'd expected.

"When you're done," he added, "select a couple of dramatic shots for the Port Angeles *Peninsula Daily News.* Offer to draft an article about the unfortunate destruction by avalanche of the historic University of Washington research station. Emphasize the extreme danger of the current snow conditions on Mount

Olympus. That should discourage hikers and anyone else who might be thinking of climbing here."

"You got your wish, Cooper. Landry's no longer a threat. But you don't have to chase everyone away. It's almost like you're glad the avalanche happened."

"I actually am," he said. "We don't need her or anyone else snooping around." He turned to see Sam glaring at him.

11

Caltech Research Site
Blue Glacier

Thursday, June 9

After Sam returned with Cooper to the operations hut, she uploaded the photographs he'd requested she send to the cartel. She attached the basic information describing the occurrence of an avalanche down the side of Panic Peak that buried the University of Washington's Research Station. Dr. Kate Landry, she explained, was the only occupant, and she escaped unharmed. Afterward, Sam emailed a photograph and press release to the newspaper in Port Angeles.

Having completed her tasks, Sam said she wanted to lie down for a few minutes to rest after all the excitement of the avalanche. She went to her personal shelter, her bedroom next to the operations hut, but instead of resting, she powered up her laptop connected to the satellite modem that Tex had given her and composed her first security alert. Sam said she was reporting a concern involving Dr. Cooper, as Tex had requested. She told him that an avalanche had occurred the night before, burying the University of Washington Research Station and that she had sent a photograph of the destruction to the cartel. Although she had no hard evidence, she thought Cooper might have had something to do with the avalanche because he had been acting nervous the night the avalanche occurred. She explained that if Dr. Landry had been seriously injured or killed, the resulting publicity and investigation by the authorities could have put the security of Cooper's geoengineering operation in jeopardy. Sam emphasized that this was only a hunch, but she thought Tex should know.

Cooper was sitting at his workstation when she returned to the operations hut, and papers were scattered across every square inch of the surface. No wonder he needed her help to get anything accomplished.

"Feeling better?" he asked in a cool voice devoid of caring.

Sam avoided looking him in the eye. "Yeah, a five-minute power nap really helps." She sat at her terminal with her back to him and returned to compiling the weather data collected the day before by the ten remote weather stations distributed around Blue Glacier.

She had mixed feelings about sending the message. She felt guilty passing on information based on a hunch, but Tex had made it clear he wanted to know if Cooper's actions attracted attention to their work. If he *had* triggered the avalanche and Dr. Landry had been killed, it would have exposed their study to outside scrutiny. And even though Dr. Landry was safe now, the whole thing could raise questions. Sam realized she'd just have to get used to the uncertain life of a spy. It certainly wasn't glamorous, and there was still the risk of getting caught.

12

National Center for Atmospheric Research
Boulder, Colorado

Thursday, June 9

G rant took a seat at the back of the small auditorium in the NCAR lab building. There were already about forty climate researchers assembled for a talk on the comparative effectiveness of violent weather warning messages sent to the public. He attended these professional briefing seminars as often as he could because it was an efficient way to learn about the issues on the cutting edge of climate science.

As he settled in, he saw Liu on the aisle one row down. He smiled and waved, and she smiled back. He realized he finally felt like he belonged in the company of these climate scientists. The turning point was when he began facilitating the small group discussions about science advocacy. Several of those people had become friends, and they'd invited him to go skiing and out to dinner.

About five minutes into the talk, his cell phone buzzed in his pocket. It was a text from Kate. "Call me. Urgent." He suddenly felt nauseous. Since she had no cell service on the glacier, something bad must have happened.

Grant texted back, "Two minutes." The feeling of nausea grew in his stomach as he rushed out of the auditorium and down the hall to his office. She picked up on the first ring when he called. "Kate, what's wrong? Where are you?"

"I'm at the airport in Port Angeles waiting for the bus to take me back home."

"Are you hurt? What happened?" He knew Kate would never abandon her glacier. It must have been something really bad.

"I'm still shaking. I needed to talk." Her voice quivered with emotion. "I'm okay, but I was nearly killed—twice."

"Oh, my God! Tell me." He'd rarely heard Kate this upset. He would have crawled through the phone to hold her if he could.

"First, Jack's helicopter iced up and we almost crashed."

Grant got up from his desk and began pacing. "How's that possible this time of year?"

"I know it seems unusual. But it can. And it did."

"But you landed safely? You weren't hurt?"

"No, we weren't hurt. Jack did an amazing job."

He could barely wait for her to tell the whole story. "Then what?"

"After the sun melted the ice, we flew to the research station."

"Okay, but you said you almost died twice."

"The second time was the worst."

Kate stopped talking for so long that Grant checked his phone to be sure they were still connected.

"I was buried in an avalanche," she finally said.

"No! How?"

"I heard it coming, ran into the station, and dove under the table. It was horrible—the shaking, the glass breaking, boards splintering. The station's completely buried. It happened last night, but I couldn't dig myself out until this morning."

Grant's legs became weak and he sat back down. He remained quiet for a long time, looking out the window while trying to figure out why her story bothered him so much. He hadn't felt this shaken since he'd gotten word that his fiancée, Megan, had drowned in a boating accident four years earlier. "Kate, I'm worried. You've always taken risks, and I admire your guts and determination, but . . ." He paused and took a deep breath.

"But what, Grant?" He heard the edge to her voice.

"I don't want to lose you." He felt his throat tighten. He honestly didn't know if he could take the uncertainty of Kate working on the glacier, especially alone and without communication.

"Okay, I get that. But do you think I was foolish to fly to the glacier?" He could hear her pushing back.

"No, you had no way of knowing about the icing conditions."

"Do you think I was wrong to check out the station before the students arrived?"

"No. In fact, that was a good idea."

"Well then, what are you saying?"

Grant couldn't come up with the words to explain the tight feeling in his gut. His eyes brimmed with tears, and he could barely talk, but he whispered, "I love you, and I can't imagine life without you. I can't wait for us to be together again." At that moment, he regretted his decision to move to Boulder. But that train of thought wasn't helping Kate. Dammit. He realized he was focused on himself and made himself shift his focus to her needs. "But I know life has no guarantees." He set his jaw and took a deep breath. "Just as you've accepted my going to Boulder, I will do everything I can to support you."

Kate was sniffling and blowing her nose. "And I love you *so much*. I wish you were here."

As Grant heard her emotion and love, his composure began to return. "What are you going to do now?"

"I've got a meeting with John Rollins, my department chair, this afternoon. We'll talk about the options."

"Any chance the station can be repaired?"

"I just sent you a photo of the station I took while waiting to get picked up at the glacier."

Grant's phone beeped and he pulled up the photo. "You survived *that*? There's nothing left but piles of snow."

"The station's there, underneath. It could be restored, but it would take a ton of work. We can't get heavy equipment up there. I doubt this can be done for this summer's research window."

"Could the students help?"

"Maybe. If they're willing to work hard for a few credits. It isn't what they signed up for, though. And besides, the university might not let them go. It's not looking good."

"Well, you've got a meeting with Rollins. See what he has to say. Find out what's possible before you assume you can't go back."

"I'll try to be flexible and optimistic." She sighed. "I've got to go. The bus is here."

"Okay. Good luck. Let me know how it goes. Talk again this evening?"

"Sure. Thanks for listening. Love you. Bye."

As he put away his cell phone, he wondered what Kate would do if she couldn't share her love for Blue Glacier with her students. Then he wondered how fast he could get a flight to Seattle.

13

Department of Atmospheric Sciences
University of Washington

Thursday, June 9

Kate was rehearsing in her mind what she would say to Dr. Rollins about the research station and avalanche as she approached his office. She knew he could be difficult and she was psyching herself up.

When she knocked on his open door, he invited her in and told her to take a seat. Dr. Rollins sat at his messy desk, but he motioned to a seat at the circular table with a view of the Seattle skyline. His office was on the top floor of the Atmospheric Sciences-Geophysics Building, and the view was spectacular. His voice was deep and strong as always, but his weary face was hiding something. He seemed to take forever rising from his desk and walking slowly to the chair beside Kate.

She could see storm clouds in the distance over the Olympics, but she wasn't there for the view. She sat on the edge of her chair and leaned forward with her elbows on the table, one heel bouncing nervously.

Rollins cleared his throat. "It's horrible about the avalanche, but I'm glad you're okay."

"It was hell, John. Thankfully, I made it inside before the wall of snow hit. The station is a wreck, with broken dishes and window glass everywhere." Kate tried to convey the urgency she felt to return to the glacier. "The north wall caved in at the top, and some snow spilled onto the upper bunks. But, thank goodness, the cables held the station to the rocks. I believe it's salvageable with some work. My students and I could make the repairs before—"

"Kate, you're not going back for a while."

An avalanche of panic plowed through her. She *had* to convince Rollins that her work must go on. "I know it will delay our getting started, but—"

"Listen to me." Rollins held up his hand like a policeman stopping traffic. "The provost and I met this morning. I'm sorry, but the university won't risk sending you and students up there again with the threat of avalanche, especially after the deaths last summer. A faculty committee needs to be convened to evaluate the risks."

Kate lurched forward in her chair. "But we have a chance to study a glacier that's stopped receding. You know how rare that is."

Rollins' back stiffened. "That may be true, but it's too dangerous."

Sensing she was losing the argument, Kate tried another tack. "We can't let Dr. Cooper from Caltech get all the credit for documenting this rare weather. UW has studied Blue Glacier for years."

"From what you've told me, he's already collected data there for months. You can't compete with that."

Kate slumped. "What am I supposed to do instead?"

Rollins paused, taking a deep breath, and looked directly at her. "We're talking about this summer, at least. The university has no choice but to pause your work on the glacier."

Kate jumped to her feet. "What? After all the years I've given to this place? Did you tell him about our contributions? What about the mammoth? Did you even *try* to go to bat for me?"

Rollins looked up at her, his face pale. "Of course I tried. It's bigger than the university. The NSF has pulled its funding. You know you're vulnerable as an associate tenure track professor using soft money from NSF to pay for part of your teaching load. But the university administration is especially worried about lawsuits if another avalanche happens while you and students are on the glacier."

"I get that, but our research on glaciers is too important to simply stop. Alpine glaciers tell us a lot about the climate. And why wasn't I part of these discussions, John? I'm the principal investigator on the project."

"You were out of town."

Kate paced to the window and back. "So the avalanche gave them the excuse they needed. That's *bullshit!*" She slammed her fist on the table, and the sharp pain of it fueled her anger. "Fixing the climate is too important for politics to interfere. I won't let it!" She leaned on the table, towering over Rollins. "They can't stop me that easily. Just watch."

She turned her back on him and stared at the rain battering the glass of the panoramic window. It was all out there—the world in peril, the climate unpredictable. And here she was butting heads with a bunch of academic bean counters safely tucked into a manmade fortress looking out at their pretty views and pretending they gave a damn about the real world.

"What will you do?" he finally asked.

A sideways smirk worked its way across her face. She belonged out there. She belonged on the glacier doing her work and making a difference. She was tired of chasing dollars, year after year. National Science Foundation indeed. NSF stood for No Science Funding. She took a deep breath and squared her shoulders. She was done with university politics, but out there, that was where she had work to do. "I'm going back to collect data on the glacier. After I clear out my office and lab, it's no longer your concern, John."

She got up from the table, turned, and charged out of the office and past his wide-eyed administrative assistant.

Kate left the building and headed for her car feeling numb, furious, and stunned. Cutting in and out of traffic, she drove to the beach on Seattle's west side where a narrow strip of sand ran for miles along Puget Sound. Walking aimlessly in the stiff sea breeze, she tried to burn off her anger so she could sort out what to do.

She raged out loud at Rollins, the university, and Congress. None of them had any clue about the damage the climate was already inflicting. Her life felt empty as she realized she could no longer impact students through the work on Blue Glacier. And what would become of her relationship with Grant? After NCAR, he planned to join her team. Now maybe he'd just stay in Boulder. She couldn't bear to lose him *and* her job.

The sunbathers and strollers who'd been staring at Kate as she muttered to herself left the beach when the late afternoon sun dipped below the hills on the west side of the sound. The wind off the water made it too cold to stay. Exhausted, Kate settled on a plan. She would set up camp on the glacier and document the abrupt cooling on Mount Olympus. She could live on savings and pay for a few helicopter trips to the glacier and back.

She'd lock up her Seattle condo, and her neighbor would care for Snowflake as she had every summer. By the time she finished her work on the glacier, the university would likely have terminated her for defying a direct order. She'd have to find something to support herself, possibly a teaching job at another college somewhere.

On her drive back to the condo, she had mixed feelings about the video call she'd arranged with Grant. She knew he'd understand her predicament and she knew he loved her, but she had no idea what his reaction would be to her plan of returning to the glacier on her own. In truth, she didn't really know if she could pull off that plan. She sighed. Her future was so uncertain.

14

Kate Landry's Condo
Seattle, Washington

Thursday, June 9 and Friday, June 10

Grant was sitting on Kate's couch waiting for her. Snowflake, having been returned by the next-door neighbor, lay curled up asleep on his lap. He'd taken an early afternoon flight from Denver to Seattle, caught a bus downtown, and let himself into her condo with her spare key. But as it began to get dark, his anticipation of a joyful reunion turned to worry. What was taking her so long?

When Kate walked through the door, she saw him and froze for a second. "Grant, my God! You're here!" She ran to the couch as he jumped up, Snowflake bounding off his lap. They embraced and he held her tight.

Neither one spoke for a minute until Kate finally said, "Now you're here, holding me, in my home. All is okay with the world. I love you so much."

"I love you too. I just didn't want you to deal with all this alone. I had to be with you." He took Kate's hand and led her to the couch, where they sat thigh to thigh. "Where have you been? You look . . ." He searched for the right word. Frankly, Kate looked like hell, but he couldn't say that to her. "You look so tired."

"It all started with my meeting with Rollins this morning after you and I talked."

"Yes, how'd that go?"

"He said I can't return to the glacier until the university forms a committee to study the risks. I told him it's critical to learn what's causing the glacier to grow."

Grant stared at her, unbelieving. "*What?*"

"He said NSF cut funding for my climate research. The university claimed fieldwork on Blue Glacier was too dangerous."

"You should fight this thing! None of that was your fault. Aren't you under contract with the university?"

"Yes, but my contract was contingent on outside funding—NSF in my case." She punched the sofa cushion. "So it looks like I'm out of a job."

"No wonder you thought your career was over."

"It was such a shock, and it felt like betrayal after all the years I devoted to U-Dub teaching and doing research. They didn't even have the courtesy to include me in the meetings before they made their decision."

Grant held Kate's hand, remaining silent as he listened.

"I was so angry I couldn't see straight. I drove over to that beach on the west side and just walked up and down for hours fuming until I started to get cold."

"Your hand is still cold." Grant wrapped his arm around Kate's shoulders and pulled her close.

"I was afraid you'd stay in Boulder permanently since I don't have a job anymore."

Grant leaned over and kissed her cheek. "I will *never* leave you." He could see she was exhausted. "Have you had anything to eat? Let's fix something. I'm starved."

Kate stared helplessly at the kitchen. "I was supposed to be on the glacier. I don't have any food."

"Then let's order takeout. How's sushi sound?"

As they dipped nori and spicy tuna rolls into soy sauce and wasabi, Grant could see the cumulative tension and fatigue from the last few days in the dark circles under Kate's eyes.

After he rinsed the empty sushi containers and dropped them in the recycle bin, he sat back down next to Kate. "You look exhausted. Let's go to bed and sort things out in the morning." Throughout the night he lay close, spooning her body as if to protect her.

———

In the morning, while Kate was out buying breakfast burritos and orange juice from the nearby deli, Grant mulled over an idea that had started to develop almost as soon as she told him about losing the funding for her work. That idea was now growing into a proposal.

They went for a walk around a lake not far from the university, and it seemed to Grant that Kate was avoiding the difficult conversation now that she might no longer have a job. When he'd asked about it, she changed the subject. He was waiting for her to bring up the topic so he could make his proposal, but even though he could be patient, they needed to talk before he had to fly back to Boulder the next day. He wondered why she was so hesitant to talk about her situation.

When they returned to Kate's condo, she brought it up herself. "Since my meeting with Rollins yesterday, I've thought a lot about what I need to do."

"So have I," Grant said as he looked hopefully into her eyes.

"It's not what you think." She took a deep breath. "I've decided to return to the glacier. Whatever's happening there is too important to leave unexplained."

Grant tried to hide his surprise and disappointment. "You've got nowhere to stay. You can't live in a pup tent on top of the mountain all summer. What if there's another avalanche?"

"You sound like my boss. *Ex*-boss."

Grant frowned. "I'm sorry, but he has a point."

Kate threw up her hands. "Do you expect me to study climate change from my condo? I've got to get out to where the climate is changing."

"Actually, Kate, I would like you to come to Boulder and live with me. There's less reason for you to stay in Seattle now." He paused, waiting for her response. When he didn't get one, he decided it might be taking time for the idea to sink in. "You could get a teaching position at CU or do research at NOAA or one of the other labs in town. It's a great place to live."

Kate got up and walked around the table. Grant couldn't quite read her expression, but then she leaned over and gave him a lingering kiss.

"Wow," he said breathlessly. "I love you too. Is that a yes?"

She sat down again, smiling. "That was because it was sweet of you to ask me, but I've made up my mind. I *have* to find out what's happened to my glacier. I've never seen conditions like this, and they may not last."

Grant knew how strong-willed Kate could be, but he was worried. "I'm afraid you're stressed by all you've been through. You need time to think before acting."

Her back stiffened and she pulled away. "I know you're trying to be helpful, but it's not working. I don't need to be protected. I need your support."

Grant reached out and took Kate's hand in both of his. "Okay. I'm sorry. I'm worried about you getting hurt or worse. But let's not argue. We've only got a few more hours before I have to go to the airport. Would you please just consider my offer? I'd love it if we could be together again."

Kate looked down at their joined hands. "I'm scared," she said in a soft voice. "Please try to understand, and don't try to talk me out of it. If I gave up on my dream, I would have nothing left. It could kill what you and I have."

Grant put an arm around her shoulder. "I'm sorry. I know this is important to you, and I'm trying to understand." Even to his own ears, it sounded a bit more hopeful than he really felt.

15

Kate Landry's Encampment
Blue Glacier

Tuesday, July 5

Kate had prepared to leave Seattle and set up her research on Blue Glacier in a blur of frenzied activity. First, she transferred personal equipment she'd used at her university lab, as well as files, to her condo. Then she assembled the basic gear and supplies she needed for weeks on the glacier. By then her living space was so cramped she asked her neighbor to take Snowflake early. Finally, she arranged for her mail to be held by the post office and made sure her utilities would be paid automatically while she was out of town.

During that time, she'd received daily phone messages and texts from Grant, and she sent him brief replies each time, telling him how busy she was and that she loved him. She'd regretted being so adamant about returning to the glacier when he'd come to support her, but she tried to stay busy and focus on getting ready. She'd needed time to prepare for her research and see what direction her life would take after the summer.

After ten days, Kate had packed her gear and supplies into her car and drove to the airport in Port Angeles, where Jack was waiting with his helicopter to fly her up to Blue Glacier. Once back on the glacier, Kate stood on the flat expanse at the top of Snow Dome surrounded by everything she and Jack had thrown randomly from his helicopter onto the snow. The cloudless sky was a deep blue, and the sunlight reflecting off the snow made her put on goggles right away and take off her jacket. She turned and told Jack to send her his invoices. He didn't need to know the university waiver she had been using to land on the glacier was no longer in effect. She could get away with a few trips, even though they were technically unauthorized.

This time Kate brought her skis, along with everything she needed for her research. After having served as captain of the ski team while an undergraduate at the Colorado School of Mines, Kate couldn't wait to exchange her clunky snowshoes for her old trusty and slightly beat-up pair of skis and the thrill of schussing through deep powder down the side of Snow Dome.

She watched the helicopter as it departed until it shrank to a dot on the horizon. For a moment she wondered if she was seeing double when a second dot appeared a few degrees to the west. Kate dug through her duffle bag, pulled out her binoculars, and focused on the object. It was much closer, and when she got it in focus, she saw it was a quadcopter drone hovering near the summit of Panic Peak. She shook her head. Cooper was spying on her. No one else was within twenty-five miles. "I don't have time for you right now," she said to Cooper's drone, "but I promise, you'll hear from me when the time is right."

She scanned the stark but familiar beauty of the surroundings. Instead of conveying a sense of peace and comfort as it always had in the past, Blue Glacier now seemed ominous. She was taking the biggest gamble of her life coming back to the glacier to spend weeks alone.

Among her new purchases for the trip was a sturdy tent, rugged enough to withstand arctic conditions and tall enough to walk in and stand upright. She erected it on the east side of the rock outcrop that held the buried research station. That would provide some shelter from the winds she expected to howl off the Pacific. She chuckled to herself, realizing it was not the pup tent Grant had imagined. This was her home and office for the next two months, so it had to be both comfortable and yet strong.

As she unrolled the bright red fabric and drove long spikes into the snow to anchor the bottom of the tent, Kate began thinking of Grant. Could they revive their relationship after the summer apart? She quickly pushed the question out of her mind. She had too much work to do.

By early afternoon, Kate had set up the compact electric generator and installed a tripod supporting the dish antenna that was aimed at the internet communication tower on Hurricane Ridge. She now had connectivity to the rest of the world when she needed it. Inside the tent she set up her cot and a camping table that served as her desk.

A deep male voice startled her. "You came back."

She poked her head out and saw Cooper standing a few feet away. "Well, if it isn't my neighbor, Dr. Cooper." Although Kate appreciated his coming to her aid after the avalanche, she still couldn't stand his arrogant attitude.

"I heard your helicopter this morning and thought I'd see what you're up to. You still planning to document the weather and snow buildup?"

"Must be one or two things left you haven't studied."

Cooper smiled at her dig. "I'm sure you're right. And you should publish your results as soon as possible. Give the world some good news amidst all the gloom and doom about climate change."

"That's not what you said the last time we talked about my research plans."

He shrugged. "I've changed my mind now that I see how determined you are."

Kate just stared at him with raised eyebrows.

"I see you're busy, but I wanted to say hi and encourage you to get the word out about the glacier's growth."

She paused, thinking about what to say next. "You mean your drone couldn't tell you what I'm up to?" She hoped to make Cooper squirm.

He didn't flinch. "Sure, I saw your tent, but I use drones mostly to document the snow buildup."

"Oh, *I* see," she said. "So you weren't really spying on me."

"Right." He looked down at his snowshoes and back at her. "When are your students coming? Is everyone staying in tents?" He was obviously trying to change the subject.

Kate knew next to nothing about Cooper, let alone whether she could trust him. But he and Sam were the only humans for miles, and they'd helped her when she needed it. So she gave him her cover story, which was partially true. "The university didn't want to expose students to the risk of avalanches. The class was cancelled."

"Why did they let *you* come then?"

"I told them how important it was to study what was causing this rare growth of a glacier." She left out the part about being told not to return.

Cooper's wrinkled forehead and half smile conveyed more questions, but she had wasted enough time. "I need to finish setting up, so I'll say goodbye." She moved toward the tent.

"See you later," he called out as he snowshoed away.

By midafternoon the internet connection worked, and her handheld radio signal was strong when she called Ben at the

Hoh Rain Forest Visitor Center. The research station was back in business with her as the sole scientist. Things were looking up.

Now Kate wanted to tell Grant she was back doing research on the glacier and sent him a text message over the internet asking him to call when he could.

Almost immediately, her laptop chirped with Grant's incoming video call. "Kate, are you okay? I've been missing you." His eyes showed concern instead of the wide-eyed warmth they normally held.

"It's good to see you, Grant. I got your messages, but I was too busy to talk much until now. I've got everything set up on the glacier."

"I knew you were busy and headed to the glacier but not much more than that."

She felt a stab of guilt and panic in her chest. "I just needed to get up here, and it took turning my whole life around to make it happen." Her face grew warm and she looked away from the screen.

"I was hoping to hear more from you. I've been trying to stay busy since we talked last, but I couldn't stop worrying."

She sighed. "I'm sorry, Grant. Right now I'm exhausted. Can we continue this tomorrow night?"

"I guess so, but we haven't really talked for over a week. I'd like to hear how you're doing. Tomorrow night then. I love you." His face disappeared from her screen.

She was annoyed. Why couldn't he be patient? She went outside and gazed up at Snow Dome and beyond to the summit of Mount Olympus. The whole scene was bathed in the orange light of the sun's last rays. But rather than the warm glow inside she usually felt this time of day, she felt totally alone in a strange and foreboding land. She zipped up the tent flap and crawled into her sleeping bag while it was still twilight. Maybe she *was* retreating from the world and from Grant, but all she wanted now was to get some rest.

Sometime in the middle of the night, Kate dreamed that her mother was still alive, sitting beside her on the porch swing at the ranch. When she looked over, her mom was hooked up to a chemo drip. Then she watched as her pale and shrunken mother lay dying in a hospital bed.

Kate woke suddenly with a tight chest. Something awful was happening to Blue Glacier. It was dying, and she couldn't do anything to stop it. The glacier had been shrinking for the entire nine years she'd been studying it. But now there was a glimmer of hope for recovery from global warming. The recent wave of cold and snow might provide a respite, if not a renewal. She wanted to believe this weather anomaly was real—a harbinger of change. If she could learn what was causing it, maybe there would be hope for her glacier and even the entire planet. As a scientist, she knew this was not a rational expectation, but it came from her heart. And as long as there was hope, she would keep trying.

16
Caltech Research Site
Blue Glacier

Tuesday, July 5

"Landry spotted our drone," Cooper said as he handed Sam a mug of coffee, keeping the other for himself. She was sitting at her work station in front of her computer monitor wearing a down vest over a flannel shirt because the shelter temperature was set at sixty degrees to keep the electronics from overheating.

"What?" Sam asked as she took the earbuds from her ears. "You said something?"

"Dammit Sam, I always have to repeat myself because you can't hear me over your music."

"Well, you've been repeating yourself for months about the security of our operation. It gets old. I need music to keep my sanity."

"We need to take precautions." Cooper ran his hand through his unkempt hair, realizing how badly he needed a haircut and a shave. "I met with Landry and she told me she spotted our drone."

"I'm not surprised. She's pretty observant, but why does that bother you so much?"

Cooper began pacing as he always did when he was anxious or excited. Recalling Faisal's last words, he said, "Every day she's on the glacier, she's a threat. She doesn't even need to discover our real objective. Just having another accident—which she seems prone to—would attract outsiders and publicity."

"Could you just hold still? It's hard to have a conversation with you moving around." Sam scrambled her hands in crazy circles to illustrate her point.

Cooper frowned and sat at his desk chair facing Sam.

"You said the avalanche would keep her away. Did she tell you why she's back?"

"Apparently, she wants to document the weather on her own. She's one stubborn lady. But her story puzzled me. She said the university wouldn't let her bring students back up because it was too dangerous. But she didn't say why they let *her* return." Cooper raised an index finger. "I'm going to call to find out what that's all about."

"Go for it." Sam reinserted her earbuds and turned back to her computer screen.

Cooper found the number of Landry's department in the UW online directory and punched it into his satellite phone. A female voice answered. "Atmospheric Sciences Department. May I help you?"

"I'm Dr. Mark Cooper from Caltech. I'd like to speak with Dr. Landry please."

"I'm sorry, she's no longer employed by the university."

"I see." He paused for a moment. "Could I speak with the head of the department?"

After being put on hold, he heard a deep voice. "John Rollins. How can I help you?"

"I'm Dr. Mark Cooper from Caltech, and I'm doing field work on Blue Glacier."

"Dr. Cooper, I understand you were asking about Dr. Landry. I'm afraid I'm not free to say any more than she no longer works here."

Cooper drummed his fingers on the desk. "Did you know that Dr. Landry is back on the glacier, claiming to be conducting a study for the university?"

"No. I haven't spoken with her since she left. But why is that a concern of yours?" Rollins sounded suspicious.

"I'm worried about her safety after the avalanche destroyed the research station."

"We were concerned too, but she's no longer affiliated here. What she does on her own is up to her. I suggest you tell her your concerns directly."

"I'll do that, then. Thanks. Goodbye." Cooper let out a contented sigh and turned to Sam. "We've got her now!"

"What?" Sam removed her earbuds and swiveled her desk chair to face Cooper. Her arms were crossed and she looked irritated.

"Landry will have to leave when the Park Service kicks her off the mountain for flying here on false pretenses."

Sam rolled her eyes. "Okay."

Cooper opened the Olympic National Park website and entered an anonymous comment, speaking it as he typed. "Dr. Kate Landry landed her chartered helicopter on Blue Glacier yesterday under a waiver for the University of Washington. She is no longer employed by the university, so her flight was illegal."

"What if they question why someone would be sending that message?" Sam asked.

"No problem. They can verify Dr. Landry's status on their own. What matters is that she'll have to leave soon because she can't get supplies. Or they might arrest her before that for flying here illegally."

"How can she leave if she can't charter a ride?"

He grunted with exasperation. "You just don't get it. That's not our problem. She could always hike out, but I'm sure the Park Service would be happy to remove her and her gear to preserve the wilderness." Cooper got up and went over to Sam. "Now that I've got that covered, how's your social media campaign?"

Sam glared at him. "I'm not some bubbleheaded undergraduate you can boss around. Have I let you down these past months?"

Cooper scowled at her but said nothing.

"Here's my latest post." Sam pointed at her monitor. "Take a look yourself. It ought to create some buzz. I'll schedule it to post hourly on social media after the next snowstorm."

Her post said that Blue Glacier was experiencing unheard of heavy snowfall in July and that the Olympic Mountains were receiving more snow than ever before recorded at this time of year. Then she ended by saying, "So much for global warming. Climate scientists are left scratching their heads."

"Not bad." Cooper stroked his stubbly chin. "The hard-core deniers will pick it up, and it's all true. It doesn't sound too extreme, which might otherwise make people suspicious."

"I've also posted the video you asked for—the one of the research station buried by the avalanche. You want to see it?"

"No. I trust you. But how close are you to having the million-follower count we talked about?"

"We're up to about seven hundred fifty thousand." Sam pointed to her screen. "And we're gaining about a thousand a week."

Cooper shook his head. "Can't you pick up the pace? I'd like us to hit the million target the cartel wanted by the time we shut down."

"I'm doing the best I can." Sam shrugged her shoulders. "We could ask some of the climate change deniers with big followings to promote our posts and encourage more followers."

"Do it. I want to keep the cartel happy. They're not going to like that Landry is back. I'll tell them we've made sure she'll be leaving again soon."

"Speaking of your cartel, I've been noticing a pattern. Every time I post about the cooling and snow buildup on Blue Glacier, someone immediately forwards it. Do you think it's your cartel?"

"Very likely. They said they would leverage our results. Your job is to get the word out. The cartel can use it however they want."

Sam brought up a screen with links to websites and turned it toward Cooper. "Here's the latest results from key word alerts. There are more articles referring to the cold weather and growth of Blue Glacier. I think our social media campaign is working."

He glanced at her screen. "That's good. I also encouraged Landry to publish her results. If she stays busy, she won't snoop into our business."

He looked over, but Sam hadn't heard the last part. She'd already shoved her earbuds back in. He threw up his arms and retreated to his workstation shaking his head.

———

Out of the corner of her eye, Sam watched Cooper's exasperated expression and retreat to his workstation. She was sick of his tantrums and realized she'd been foolish to have had reservations about spying on him for the cartel. It was time to send another security warning to Tex. Cooper had gone ballistic over Dr. Landry's return to the glacier, and within half an hour, he'd contacted both the University of Washington and the Park Service to complain.

Pretty soon everyone in the State of Washington would be wondering what was happening on Mount Olympus.

"Hey, Coop. I gotta go back to my shelter for a bit," she called out, trying to sound nonchalant. "Be back in a sec."

Cooper growled. "I need you to integrate all the weather station data. Can't it wait?"

"No, actually." Sam got up from her computer station. "Female stuff." Cooper blushed, and she turned her back on him just in time to hide her grin.

When Sam charged into her personal shelter, she was on a mission to contact Tex about Cooper's latest outburst. It had actually worried *her*. But as she glanced around, she had a brief moment of guilt about the state of her personal space. Her bedding was a balled-up mess, some clothes were hung over the back of a chair, and other clothes were scattered across the floor next to her open duffle. The small desk was cluttered with her personal items—deodorant, toothpaste, hairbrush—and a few quartz crystals she'd chipped from rocks on the side of Mount Olympus. Her mother would never have approved of the way she kept her room. But, hey, this was her space on the side of a mountain.

Sam opened her laptop, which was still connected to the satellite modem, and logged onto the special email app she used to communicate with Tex.

Sam told Tex that she was concerned that Cooper was losing it and was ranting about Landry's return to the glacier after he was sure that the avalanche had chased her off for good. She also told him about Cooper's call to the University of Washington and anonymous message left with the Park Service. She ended by saying that Cooper's contacts were threatening the security of the operation.

She was about to return to the operations hut when her Wi-Fi enabled cell phone rang. It was her mother, calling out of the blue. Now Sam felt guilty because she hadn't called in a month, but she didn't have time to visit now.

"Hi, Mom, what's up?" She asked, trying to keep her impatience from her voice.

"Hi, sweetie! Are you doing okay? I keep thinking about you alone with your adviser on the glacier. You told me . . . I'd be getting cash . . . my mortgage and expenses."

Sam detected a bit of slurring in her mother's faltered speech. "Mom, have you been drinking?"

"Sweetie, don't get mad. I've just had a little to calm down."

Sam threw up her arm. "Mom, that will kill you just like it did Dad. You've got to stop." No response. "When I get paid, you'll get the cash. But it won't be for a little while longer. I need to finish my work up here on the glacier first."

"When will that be?"

"In a few weeks. Can you make ends meet until then?"

"I guess so, but you know how tight things have been since Papa died."

That was the hundredth time she had said this. Sam didn't respond.

"Oh, I wanted to tell you. A nice man stopped by. Introduced himself. Said you and he had met."

Sam's breathing stopped for a moment. "What did he look like?"

"He was tall and had blue eyes. Looked like a cowboy with his Western shirt and cowboy hat."

"Was his name Tex Stone?" She felt her face flush with anger. That would be like him—inserting himself in her family's affairs.

"Yes, that's it. So you *do* know him." Her voice sounded more cheerful.

"What did he want?" Sam was getting annoyed at her mother's naïveté and drinking, but she was furious at Tex.

"He wanted to know my finances, like how big my mortgage is and how much Social Security I get. Seemed rude asking, but he knew you. Thought it was okay if I told him."

She couldn't believe what she was hearing and felt panic. And she had a bitter taste in her mouth. "Mom, I know who he is, but you shouldn't give out that information to strangers." She wondered how her mother could be so gullible. "Please, from now on, don't assume it's okay." Sam took a deep breath to calm herself. "Okay?"

"Sure, Sam. I'm sorry. Won't do it again. Miss you. Can you stop by when you're done up there? I need the company."

"That sounds good, Mom. Like I said, just a few more weeks. I'll give you a call as soon as I know. Love you. Bye."

"Bye, dear."

Sam was worried about her mom, but the way Tex and the cartel were intruding in her personal life was frightening. Her face burned with rage. It was one thing for Tex to set up a trust for her mother, but showing up on her mother's doorstep was not only uncalled for, it was completely unacceptable. She opened her laptop, connected to the satellite modem, and typed, "Tex, stay away from my mother. Totally bogus! Sam."

She stormed back to the operations hut, mad and worried about how much the cartel and Tex, in particular, were getting involved in her personal life. But as soon as she walked through the door of the hut and while she was still shielded by the canvas storm flap, she overheard Cooper addressing Tex on the satellite phone, so she stood and listened.

"Everything is going according to plan, Tex," Cooper said. "We've collected the data we need to demonstrate the effectiveness of our geoengineering technology." He paused. "No, we haven't caused it to snow yet, but it's still early in July." There was another pause. "Yes, our security protocols are holding. The only exception is that Dr. Landry has returned, but I've taken care of that. She'll have to leave once her food runs out." After the next pause, Cooper's voice rose with agitation. "How? I notified the Park Service of her unauthorized presence on the glacier. I could tell from my drone that the amount of supplies she brought was limited."

Sam could tell from Cooper's side of the conversation that Tex wasn't letting on that he already knew the things she'd told him in her email. If Cooper thought she was passing information to the cartel, her work with him would come to an abrupt halt.

"I suppose there *is* a slight risk," Cooper admitted, "but I sent the notification anonymously." There was another pause. "No, I can't guarantee they won't get suspicious." Cooper raised his voice. "What am I supposed to do? Let her stay here and discover what we've done?"

Now there was a long pause while Cooper listened to Tex. "No, I don't know what caused the avalanche." Then Cooper shouted so loud she could have heard him from inside her shelter. "That's ridiculous! I was in our research station during the avalanche. You can ask Sam. She was here."

She could hear Cooper's feet pacing the plywood floor. "Are you threatening me?"

Whatever Tex said during the long pause must have scared Cooper because the next thing he said was, "Yes, sir." Then he dropped to nearly a whisper that Sam could barely hear. "I will, sir. No, sir. I'm sorry. Bye."

She wondered what Tex had said to Cooper. He had the biggest ego in the world, but Tex had said something to elicit an apology.

Sam entered the room just as Cooper dropped into his chair and lowered his head. When he looked up at her, his eyes were wide with fear.

"Did you hear me on the phone?"

"A little."

"That was the cartel. I told them Landry was back, but they were being . . . unreasonable." When he threw the papers from his desk onto the floor, Sam just stood and stared. "I can't wait to get off this damn mountain, but we haven't met our goals yet."

"I agree. I've been cooped up here too long. But what happens if we bail or fail?"

"You don't want to know what Tex just threatened." Cooper looked more frightened than Sam had ever seen him and turned away from her. "We don't get paid for one thing."

"So this whole winter up here was a waste?"

"Not if we can make it snow like we promised. We've got to make sure Landry doesn't get suspicious. We're creating conditions up here unlike anything she would ever have seen before."

Sam sat down across from Cooper when she realized the dilemma they both faced. "Satisfying your commitment to the cartel could raise Landry's curiosity and suspicion about what you and I are doing."

"Bingo," Cooper said, swiveling his chair away from Sam and toward his computer screen.

Sam felt her stomach sink and thought she might throw up.

17

Lower Blue Glacier
Olympic National Park

Wednesday, July 6

Kate pointed her ski tips down the steep slope of Snow Dome and took off on her way to the lower glacier with weather instruments and tower sections strapped to her backpack. She welcomed the thrill of speed and the wind on her face. It felt good to do something physical after the stress of her brief conversation with Grant the previous night and waking up from that weird dream about her mother's death.

After skirting far around Cooper's encampment, she skied fast through graceful arcs, her boots and skis held tight together, until the slope became more gradual and ended on the flat surface of the lower glacier. Continuing down the more gradual slope, Kate finally arrived near the tip of the lower glacier where it narrowed and Glacier Creek began its turbulent flow out from under the ice.

Soon she stood about a hundred yards up from the glacial tip and took in the stunning view of the dark-green forest below the glacier. After installing weather instruments on a tower that would transmit data to her base camp, Kate still wanted to experience the weather conditions firsthand at that location before logging them remotely.

As she faced up the gradual slope of the lower glacier behind her, she detected a cool, gentle breeze on her cheeks—the katabatic wind, also known as drainage wind. She made a mental note to tell her glaciology students that katabatic winds form when glacial ice cools the air above it, and because cold air is denser than the surrounding air, it flows downhill due to gravity. With a start, she remembered she wouldn't be teaching that class, not anytime in the foreseeable future, anyway. The loss of her teaching job hit her hard.

Looking up to the top of the tower, she saw the spinning cups of the anemometer responding to the breeze she felt. The anemometer display in Kate's hand indicated a steady flow of eight miles an hour.

Satisfied that the weather instruments were working properly, Kate inflated a weather balloon using a helium canister she had brought and unrolled a tether attached to the balloon. When the balloon rose to full height, her recording equipment measured the wind speed and temperature at six, nine, and twelve meters above the ice.

Stunned by the results, she blurted out loud, "Amazing!" The readout showed that the wind flowing down the glacier encompassed all three layers—up to the nearly forty feet at the top. Instead of a warm valley wind blowing over the glacier in the opposite direction creating turbulence that melted the ice, the surface of the glacier was shielded from the warm air by a thick blanket of cold that minimized the effects of global warming.

She felt encouraged. These results suggested that Blue Glacier stood a chance of retaining much of the new snow. It was as though nature's air conditioning kept the surface of the lower glacier cool. Studies had established that glaciers created a unique microclimate that significantly modified how they were affected by the broader weather and climatic environment surrounding them. For the first time, Kate let herself believe she now had evidence that the new snow had a chance of lasting the summer and into the next year.

She looked around for the ablation line—where the new snow overlay gave way to the bare ice below it—but there was no line, another sign that the glacier might be growing. Fresh snow covered the ice surface all the way down to the tip, confirming what she had seen a couple of weeks earlier from the helicopter. Since this fresh snow was so white, it reflected almost all the sunlight hitting it. In past years, the old, exposed snow and ice became covered with dust blowing up from the valley below and with patches of the red watermelon snow algae. Both dust and algae lowered the reflectivity, which scientists called the albedo, and led to more rapid melting.

Excited to think the glacier was growing for the first time in decades, she threw her hands into the air and drank it all in. It was the first good news she'd had in weeks, and it deserved a celebration. She was already formulating the words in her head for a paper to announce this to the scientific community. But her excitement was tempered by a nagging doubt: Although she could describe what was happening, she couldn't account for it.

She snapped her boots into the bindings and skied down to near the tip, being careful not to slide too close to the edge and into the ice-cold water rushing from under the ice into Glacier Creek. She spotted the crumpled remains of Cooper's remote weather station where Jack's helicopter had smashed it after struggling with the weight of ice. The case was cracked open and electronic components were scattered across the snow.

Although it had been a life-or-death decision to put down where Jack did, she still felt bad about setting back Cooper's science. But if his goal was to record the weather conditions on the glacier, why hadn't he replaced these instruments to ensure the continuity of their record? Was his story actually a cover for something else? Kate got a chill down her spine thinking of Cooper's habit of spying on her. Was he watching her now?

18

Caltech Research Site
Blue Glacier

Wednesday, July 6

Wearing a parka over her pajamas, Sam trudged across the snow to the central operations hut. To her surprise, Cooper was already at his computer. "Good morning," she mumbled as she walked past him to the kitchen area, where she poured a cup of coffee.

"Morning. You slept in, I see." Cooper sat at his terminal watching the video feed from one of his drones.

Sam frowned. "Give me a break. It's only eight."

"*I've* been up since daybreak tracking Landry. I followed her ski run from her camp down to the tip of the lower glacier using a drone. She's pretty fast. Funny to watch her swing wide around our camp to keep us from seeing her."

"Do you realize you're fixated on her every movement of every day? You're becoming obsessed. You realize that watching her isn't going to keep her from figuring out what we're doing up here." Though she didn't say it, Sam wondered if Cooper might be attracted to Kate Landry after all the time they'd lived in isolation.

"It can still give us a clue about what she's up to. We're screwed if she discovers our climate engineering technology. We just can't let down our guard."

"Oh, brother." Sam rolled her eyes and went over to Cooper's work station. "Now I'm curious. What *is* she doing?" She looked over his shoulder.

"Setting up some instruments." He zoomed the image showing Kate standing next to a metal case with switches and dials mounted on a tripod.

"Is that all? I swear, Cooper, you're turning into a stalker. Give Dr. Landry a break. She's trying to reduce global warming, just like we are. She just lacks your engineering savvy." Sam had learned quickly that stroking Cooper's ego helped make things tolerable. Life with Cooper had gotten old months before, but she'd remained in spite of the challenges because of the generous pay and the trust the cartel had set up to care for her alcoholic mother.

"I'll take that as a rare compliment from you. I left some bagels and cream cheese for you in the kitchen if you want. They're a few days old, but the last until our next helicopter grocery run. After breakfast we need to resupply our cloud seeding generators."

Sam prepared to launch the quadcopter drones, an activity she'd been doing every few days since she joined Cooper at the site in January. Cooper had positioned six cloud seeding generators along the mountain ridges west of Mount Olympus in September. She opened a topographic map on one of the three monitors on her desk and examined the red dots that indicated the locations of the generators. "I'm ready to deploy the drones. Let's go."

They left the shelter, each holding the handle of a large, hard-shell case and walked around to a wooden platform at the north end of the hut, where they set their cases in the snow. Cooper opened the first case, lifted the quadcopter drone it contained, and set it carefully on the platform. He looked admiringly at the drone of his design. That was one more example, Sam had noticed, of how Cooper loved to savor his technological creations.

Some people expressed themselves through works of art. Cooper achieved creative satisfaction through his inventions.

The platform had a hole to accommodate an aluminum cylinder, which was stored there. He retrieved the cylinder and fastened firmly to three grippers on the underside of the drone. Then he pressed a small switch on the drone's underside, and a green light came on after a few seconds, telling him this quadcopter was ready to fly.

"After you launch, I'll give you the signal when the next drone is ready." He held up a transceiver.

Sam went inside to her workstation and moved her cursor over the first of the six red dots on the map. She picked up her transceiver and asked, "All clear?"

"Clear," came Cooper's reply over the speaker.

She felt excitement and anticipation every time she did this. She clicked her mouse, and a loud buzzing sound came from outside the shelter as the four propellers on the quadcopter began to spin simultaneously. She heard the drone depart to fly up the side of Snow Dome to the first cloud seeding generator located on the side of a peak about two miles to the west of Mount Olympus. Then she loaded a graphic dashboard program on a second of her three monitors, displaying the instrument readings and controls associated with the silver iodide generator where the drone was headed.

After tracking the first drone, a flashing button on her monitor told her that Cooper had the second drone in position and turned on. Once he'd confirmed he was ready and clear of the whirling blades, Sam launched the second quadcopter to fly to a second silver iodide generator. Twenty minutes later, the first drone returned, hovered over the launching platform, and landed.

It would have been impossible to service the cloud seeding equipment any other way.

By the end of two hours, Cooper and Sam had serviced all six generators, which communicated over a satellite channel that they were primed for the next storm. Sam had taken charge of deploying the quadcopter drones, and it had become so routine that it was no longer a rewarding challenge. She couldn't wait to get off the glacier and leave their confining space and lifestyle.

Cooper came inside, bringing a swirl of cold air with him. "We're ready to seed the next storm front, but now I've lost track of Landry." He took off his parka and hung it up, shaking his head. "She's probably back at her camp by now. I'll be glad when she's gone."

"Like I keep saying, Cooper, just spying on Landry isn't going to protect the security of our operation. You'd better be right about how you've designed your equipment to be hard to detect."

19

Kate Landry's Encampment
Blue Glacier

Wednesday, July 6

Breathless, Kate stood on the summit of Panic Peak and looked down at her snowshoe tracks. They led down to her camp, where she'd exchanged her skis for snowshoes before making the climb with a second remote weather station strapped to her backpack frame. Now at the top, she took in the 360-degree view of the Olympic Mountains with steep slopes dropping off at her feet on three sides and a near vertical face of hundreds of feet to the north. She took a minute to catch her breath and enjoy the view of the Hoh River. The rushing sound of fast-moving water over rocks was clear and distinct, even though the river was several miles and thousands of vertical feet below.

She hoisted the instrument package, about the size of a small microwave oven but much lighter, onto a platform mounted atop a rugged tripod she'd set up. The mast holding the anemometer was not as tall as the one on the lower glacier because the sloping terrain on all sides of the peak gave it good exposure to the wind. Then she fastened three nylon cords from the base of the tripod to solid rock anchors as defense against the fierce gale-force winds she expected there.

"Let's fire this thing up," she said out loud and flipped a couple of switches on the panel on the side of the case. Three indicator lights flashed red as the diagnostic program started. After a few seconds, each light turned green, indicating that the systems were functioning properly.

Satisfied that the two sources of local weather data were adequate for now—one station at the tip of the lower glacier and one high on the upper glacier—Kate felt prepared to monitor the storms when they appeared. The coverage would be a bit sparse, but she would have all the data she would need from the top and bottom of the glacier: temperature, wind speed, barometric pressure, precipitation, and cloud cover. She felt confident she could document the basic parameters of storms as they formed and moved across the mountain.

But just as she was about to climb back down the side of Panic Peak to her camp, she heard what sounded like a swarm of bees. She snatched binoculars from her backpack and aimed them just in time to identify the source of the sound. It came from one of Cooper's drones with a gray cylinder hanging down from its center. She tracked it with the binoculars as it sped past her, headed west. Cooper must not have realized she was there because the drone flew on a straight course, apparently on a mission. After a couple of minutes, it stopped over a prominent ridge about two miles away and dropped out of sight behind a grove of trees which lined the top of a ridge.

What was Cooper up to? She kept the binoculars focused on the ridge, and after about two minutes, the drone climbed straight up and began flying back toward her along the path it had just taken. This time the cylinder was missing. Interesting. The drone must have been on some kind of a delivery run. There was something over on that ridge, and she needed to know what it was.

She studied the terrain from where she stood. It looked rugged and way too risky to hike there. Mount Olympus plummeted about two thousand feet down to White Glacier from her camp and then rose up almost as far to the ridge where the drone had landed on the far side. There was no way to get there on foot. She'd have to take Jack's helicopter.

While making the easy hike down to her tent from the summit, her thoughts turned to Grant. She'd been too absorbed in solving her own logistical problems over the past few days to have more than the brief conversation with him she'd had the previous day. She knew he was just trying to be helpful and keep their relationship intact under difficult conditions, and a small stab of guilt returned. At least they'd planned to talk that evening.

Kate double-checked the weather instruments and then snowshoed back down to her tent, where she studied her topographic map of Olympic National Park to see what the terrain was like where the drone had landed. Remote and rugged was her conclusion. There were no roads or even hiking trails leading to the ridge on the back side of Mount Tom. What reason could Cooper possibly have for delivering a mysterious gray cylinder to that out-of-the way spot? The more times she encountered Cooper's activities on the glacier, the more questions they raised. This time she thought she'd seen a clue that might tell her his true purpose for enduring a hellish winter on the side of the mountain. It would be worth the price of another helicopter ride to reveal what he was really up to.

As Kate prepared her dinner of ramen noodles and beef jerky, she looked forward to telling Grant about the drone. She liked sharing her day with him, as long as he didn't second-guess her judgment.

At eight o'clock sharp, she initiated the video call but got the message, "Internet Connection Too Slow." She tried again five minutes later, and every fifteen minutes after that for an hour. Then she tried audio-only, thinking the video required too much bandwidth, but no luck. She felt like crying from frustration.

When she finally wanted to take the time for video communication with Grant, she couldn't. Hopefully, an email would get through. Kate emailed Grant that she was sorry her internet was too slow to connect with video or audio, but the email connection seemed okay. She wrote that she had seen a quadcopter drone carrying a metal canister that afternoon while she was installing a remote weather station on Panic Peak. She described how it had flown past her, hovered, landed, and returned on the same path without the canister. Admitting she found it strange, she asked if he could talk with one of his contacts at NCAR to see if there was anything unusual about the weather patterns associated with Mount Tom. She wrote that she was suspicious that what she'd seen had something to do with the snow buildup on Mount Olympus and suggested that they plan to talk the following evening if the internet connection would let them.

20

National Center for Atmospheric Research
Boulder, Colorado

Thursday, July 7

When Grant checked his personal email at home before leaving for work in the morning, there was a message from Kate. He was sorry the internet connection had been too slow for them to video conference or even talk without the video, but he was relieved to hear from her and happy to be able to help. When he got to his office, he sent Kate a brief email. "I'll see what I can find out re. Mount Tom weather patterns."

That noon in the cafeteria he asked Liu to join him for lunch to talk about some weather research. Liu took her responsibility about combatting climate change seriously, but her caring extended far beyond her job. She met frequently with service clubs and other civic groups to suggest ways they could help save the planet from the effects of climate change.

Grant steered them to one of the tables for two and began by saying, "You may recall my friend, Dr. Kate Landry, a glaciologist studying what is happening to Blue Glacier in Washington State." He hesitated, not sure how much to say about their relationship, especially now that it was strained. "We met last summer when I was observing her University of Washington student team for a NASA study. We've become friends."

Grant looked away as he realized he wasn't quite sure what his relationship with Kate was becoming now that she was off on her rogue research on Blue Glacier. He felt his face turn hot and wondered if Liu was gauging his body language. Struggling to regain his composure, he finally said, "She's actually living in a research camp on the glacier on the side of Mount Olympus this summer. The Olympics have had unseasonably cold weather and frequent storms. Kate wants to know if you could review recent weather data to see if you spot anything unusual in that part of the country."

"I've visited that national park. Beautiful country," Liu replied. "When did the unusual weather start?"

"Around last September."

"And it's continued up to now?"

"Yes. There's been an intense storm every couple of weeks. She'd like to know, in particular, if there is anything detectable on Mount Tom, the mountain west of Mount Olympus."

A large tour group of elementary children surged into the cafeteria, and the noise level made it hard to keep talking. Liu looked over at the kids and then back at Grant. "I think our lunch time is over." She raised her voice to be heard. "But I'm happy to take a look at the recent weather data in the Olympics. It shouldn't take long." She stood up and picked up her tray. "I'll let you know if I find anything."

Grant followed her to the recycling station where they composted unused food and left their plates and flatware in tubs. Once they were outside the cafeteria in the much quieter corridor, Liu turned to face him. "I hope you and Kate can work out whatever's going on between you."

Grant froze. "Is it that obvious?"

She leaned over and said softly, "It's written all over your face."

———

Late that afternoon, Liu called Grant to say she had something to show him. When he arrived at her office, she positioned the monitor on her desk so Grant could see it. "Take a look at this. Here's a video of satellite images of the most recent storm blanketing most of the Olympics." Using her pen as a pointer, she moved it from left to right as she said, "Notice how the bands of clouds move from west to east." Then she tapped her pen on distinct white blobs. "But six spots of higher density snow immediately to the west of Mount Olympus and over Mount Tom appear to be fixed. They don't follow the cloud bands on their eastward path. Kate should probably check them out."

"Can you give me the coordinates of those locations?"

She smiled. "Of course."

"Any idea what might be causing them?"

"They don't seem natural. If I had to guess, I'd say something on the ground is increasing the intensity of the radar reflections. Maybe some kind of cloud seeding. I already checked with the folks here who are involved with such experiments in Wyoming and Montana. They haven't heard about anything going on in Washington State, and they would probably know."

"This is helpful, Liu. Thanks." Grant stood up to leave. "Let me know if you spot anything else."

"I did find a pattern that is even more puzzling."

Grant sat back down. "Like what?"

"NOAA maintains a database of ocean conditions from a network of anchored buoys off the West Coast. Beginning last fall and continuing through the most recent readings, the ocean temperatures have been consistently lower than normal—three to five degrees centigrade. I can't tell what's causing it, but that could explain why the Olympics are getting snow from those Pacific storms."

"Interesting. Another piece to the puzzle."

"Tell Kate that without the regional cooling, we'd expect to see rainfall instead of snow. Something else is causing the snow at this time of year."

"I'll pass that along too. Thanks so much."

Grant planned to talk to Kate that night if her internet connection would even allow them to talk. He still felt worried about their connection, but he was excited to talk with her about what he'd learned. He was starting to have the dreaded sense of walking on eggshells with Kate, which was something he never wanted to happen.

At seven o'clock on the dot, he initiated a video call to Kate. The connection worked, but barely. Her face was a bit frozen, but he could hear her clearly when she said hello.

"Hi, Kate. I can hear you as long as we don't get cut off completely. You hearing me okay?"

"Sure. Glad the connection is working tonight. Were you able to find out anything about the weather over Mount Tom?"

He took a deep breath before answering. "Before we get into that, I'd like to talk about us. I can't find my way back to you if you aren't in the room with me."

The distorted image of Kate's face flickered twice, as if it were about to disappear. Then the signal cleared.

"What do you mean?"

"You were making major changes to your life and taking risks, but you didn't talk to me about it. You didn't even ask me to tell you what I thought."

She moved closer to her laptop camera and shook her head. "I told you I had to do this, and now I'm here. So let's move on." Kate's face froze again on Grant's screen, and this time the face was frowning.

"For the time being, let's just agree to disagree on that," he replied. An ache burrowed into his chest, but he ignored it and arranged his face to appear unconcerned. "I've got an answer to your question."

"Tell me what you've got."

"It turns out you were right about something unusual on Mount Tom. I asked Liu to look for clues in her data."

Kate raised her eyebrows. "Who's Liu?"

"You remember. She's one of the scientists in our building I introduced you to when you were visiting. She's an expert at modeling the effects of geoengineering on climate."

Kate nodded. "I remember. What did she find?"

"Her satellite imagery suggests the storms and snow buildup on Mount Olympus aren't natural. I'm emailing you the coordinates of six sources of especially high cloud density that you might want to explore. They're fixed points that don't move with the passing clouds."

"That's great. I'll check it out. Thanks."

He wasn't ready to hang up. "There's something else you should look into. Why did it start getting colder last September? Liu said that if the temperature hadn't dropped, you'd be getting rain instead of snow."

"Did she say what's causing it?"

"No. That's up to you to figure out."

"Okay. Thanks. I'm glad we could talk tonight, even if the connection isn't strong. But listen, I'm exhausted. I need to go. I really appreciate your help. Take care, Grant."

Grant's screen went blank. Take care? What happened to the "I love you" she would say every night? He slammed the lid of his laptop shut. The internet wasn't the only weak connection. He knew she had a lot on her plate and must be hurting from losing her job and connection to students, but he didn't understand why she was was being so distant with him. He was happy to support her as one scientist to another, but he longed for the emotional closeness that had come easily before she returned to the glacier.

Grant stepped outside. His rental cottage in Chautauqua at the base of the Flatirons, the slanted slabs of rock that were a Boulder landmark, was homey and comfortable, but it lacked air conditioning. The summer heat forced him outside when it became uncomfortably stuffy, and he thought about whether global warming had a part in that. He'd been told that many houses built in the eighties and earlier had no air conditioning because it hadn't been deemed necessary. That had changed. Looking up at the Flatirons, where he and Kate had climbed, often lifted his spirits. But not this time.

21

Kate Landry's Encampment
Blue Glacier

Friday, July 8

Early in the morning, Kate called Jack to schedule a time to fly over the spot where she'd seen the drone land. It matched one of the coordinates Grant had given her.

"Hasn't the Park Service contacted you?" he asked when she identified herself.

"No. Why should they?"

"Someone from the headquarters in Port Angeles told me the U-Dub waiver for flying you into the park has been revoked."

"What? What's the problem?" Kate hoped the National Park Service hadn't found out. Especially Ben. He'd be angry and disappointed.

"They heard you don't work for the university anymore. Is that true?"

Kate hesitated. "Well, yes. I didn't think it mattered." Actually, she had hoped no one would notice.

"It matters a lot. Without that waiver I could lose my pilot's license if I land up there."

"I'm sorry, Jack. I didn't know that." Kate rested her forehead in her hand on the table. "They should blame me, not you. The university fired me ten days ago. This may be my only chance to document the reversal of global warming, and I couldn't have gotten here with all my gear without your help."

He sighed. "Maybe try calling them. Work something out. I can't even help you leave. Good luck."

Kate sat in her tent with her head in her hands, reeling from the news. She knew she had taken a risk, but it was still a shock, and it left her with a huge problem. Not only was she unable to fly to the site she needed to check out, but the food and supplies she'd brought would only last another week. She was counting on Jack's flights to keep her supplied for the rest of the summer. How did the Park Service find out about her situation?

Panic rose and her chest tightened, but she pushed it away. She'd make every minute count of what little time she had left, beginning with climbing over to where the mysterious spots on the weather radar were located. The drone flight and satellite imagery told her someone was messing with the weather. To prove that Cooper was responsible she needed the evidence that could only be found on the side of Mount Tom. The challenge would be getting there and back without killing herself. She'd deal with the Park Service later.

Kate packed enough energy bars, beef jerky, and water to last a whole day. She didn't know what she'd be up against, but she needed to maintain her strength. Anticipating some serious mountaineering, she packed crampons for her boots, along with her ice ax, and strapped on her snowshoes.

She spent two hours getting over Snow Dome, through the pass leading to the cirque, and then climbing to the saddle between West Peak and Middle Peak, where the mountainside dropped precipitously to the west. Stopping, she studied the snow chute leading down from where she stood to a narrow, rocky ledge that ran between Mount Olympus and the side of Mount Tom. The snow above the ledge sloped so steeply that a few rocks that had fallen from the summit left skid tracks down the incline.

When she saw what she was up against, she almost turned back. It looked too dangerous, even after her years of mountaineering experience, but she felt compelled to identify what was on the other side of Mount Tom. From here it seemed so close.

She buckled on her crampons and started to inch down the steep incline, jabbing the point of her ice ax into the snow at her side for support. Her boots slid down several inches with each stride. When the entire slab surrounding her broke free and started to drop, she screamed, "Oh, my God!"

As her feet dropped out from under her, Kate moved her arms and legs in a swimming motion, attempting to stay on top of the fast-moving snow and avoid being buried and suffocated. Snow covered her head more than once, and the freezing powder forced its way into her nose and mouth, but each time, she strained to lift her head and shoulders, gasping for air.

Speeding down the slope, she lost her grip on her ice ax and it flopped wildly, held by the strap around her wrist, several times bumping her shoulder, perilously close to hitting her in the head. She tried to grab hold of the ax, her only hope, but the force of the massive snow rolled and flipped her over so the handle kept bouncing out of reach. As she saw the rock ledge approaching, she imagined glancing off and continuing to freefall onto White Glacier, a thousand feet further down.

Just then, her gloved hand caught the ice ax, and she wrestled it across her chest. She rolled onto her stomach and planted the full weight of her body over the pick end of the ax head while digging her toes into the torrent of moving snow.

But even in the self-arrest position, she couldn't stop her down-hill momentum. She was swept along helplessly by the roaring mass, headed toward the cliff at its steepest point. Frantically, she kicked with her legs and dug in with the ice ax to steer as best she could, maneuvering toward the edge of the moving cloud of snow. She hit the rock ridge with such force that it knocked the wind out of her, but the pick of her ice ax snagged a crevice in the rock and kept her from going over the edge.

She lay still on her stomach for several minutes catching her breath, feeling her arms and legs for injuries, and trying to assess her situation. This climb was crazy—more dangerous even than it had appeared from above. After a few minutes, she crawled to a level spot on the ridge, where she sat to figure out what to do next.

A narrow knife-edge of rock ran nearly horizontally for several hundred yards from the side of Mount Olympus, where she sat, to the side of Mount Tom. If she could cross this narrow strip, she could put on the snowshoes again and traverse around the back side of the mountain to the spot she had marked on her topo map. She'd figure out later how to get back.

Mount Tom dropped steeply to the south and down to another valley below, so she had to avoid climbing too far in that direction. The west side where she was headed sloped more gradually and was covered by a sparse but expansive forest of spruce.

It took Kate the better part of an hour to cross the dangerous ridge and hike to the west side where her GPS told her she should be near the spot exhibiting one of the shadows on the radar imagery.

After searching back and forth through the trees, Kate spotted something that looked out of place. Partially hidden behind a dense grove of firs and pines and covered by snow, an object with clean metallic lines contrasted with its surroundings. She'd found it! A large oblong tank, like a residential propane tank, was partially hidden under snow and was painted with camouflage colors to blend into its forest setting. Its appearance matched that of the cloud seeding devices she'd seen on the internet. A burner with a vertical column like a smokestack appeared to be designed to seed the clouds by producing microscopic particles that supercooled water vapor would freeze onto, forming snowflakes.

A platform with a hole in the center was mounted to the side of the device where Kate guessed the drone landed to deliver its cylinder payload. And there, sitting upright, was the very cylinder she had seen attached to the drone as it flew past her the day before. A few feet away stood an antenna tower she guessed Cooper was using to send and receive signals for controlling the cloud seeding equipment.

"I've got him now!" Kate said out loud as she snapped photos from different angles to document the evidence for how Cooper was modifying the weather. She was a bit concerned that he might have some kind of surveillance equipment and was watching her. And what if one of his drones arrived while she was there?

As she took one picture after another, she stopped thinking about Cooper as the true implications of what she was recording sank in. At first, she felt vindicated because it confirmed that the massive snow buildup was artificial and Cooper was a fraud. But in spite of her suspicions, she had hoped that somehow all the new snow she had observed since returning to the glacier was natural, that it was real and represented a true, if temporary, reprieve from the relentless increase of global temperatures.

Kate felt her emotions well up. The rush of relief from coming close to death and gratitude for having survived was displaced by anger. Cooper had been lying to her from the start. She was furious at him. He knew that the unusual weather was his doing, yet he pretended he was just as surprised as her and was simply documenting the weather. He'd been playing her all along.

Her fury turned to hot tears streaming down her cheeks. She had so wanted to believe that her Blue Glacier had a future. Unlike the dispassionate scientist she always aspired to be, Kate felt heartbroken and limp. She collapsed on the snow among the trees and sobbed in waves of grief. After a few minutes, she looked around and began to think more rationally. Realizing she had completed what she had come for and collected photographic evidence of Cooper's plot to change the weather, her challenge now was climbing back to her camp safely.

It would be difficult, if not deadly, to attempt to climb up the steep snow chute she had just come down. So after studying her topo map, she found a route around the south side of Mount Olympus, across two smaller glaciers, and through Glacier Pass between Hoh Glacier and Lower Blue. This route would be longer, and she wondered if it would be less dangerous. She put on her snowshoes and started out in that direction.

While slogging through the deep powder, Kate's scientific mind couldn't let go of a nagging concern. She had discovered Cooper's hidden cloud seeding equipment, but seeding could only enhance the productivity of *existing* clouds and not *cause* the storms in the first place.

Over the past year, Blue Glacier experienced more frequent storms and average air temperatures about twenty degrees Fahrenheit lower than normal. Those conditions reflected a buildup of moisture and changes to temperature and humidity usually associated with low pressure systems. She knew of no other instance of man-made weather modification that would produce these conditions. As a result, she considered that much of the unusual weather must have occurred naturally, in spite of

Cooper's storm-enhancing equipment. She needed to continue to search for *all* the factors causing the heavy snowfall. She hated the feeling of being torn between hope and disappointment.

Now that she knew at least some of the changes in conditions on Blue Glacier were man-made, her research would take on a totally different slant Although Cooper continued to hide critical information, she now had the upper hand when she next encountered him and his arrogant attitude.

After Kate's close call getting to Mount Tom, the hike around the base of Mount Olympus and through Glacier Pass to lower Blue Glacier was a long slog with her bruised and tired muscles. Fortunately, the route was relatively flat with most of the climbing at the end, up Snow Dome from lower Blue Glacier to the research station, something she had climbed many times.

When Kate finally made it back to her encampment in the late afternoon, her little tent looked cozy and welcoming. She had lost some of her fierce determination through her ordeal, and it made her miss Grant and his efforts to take care of her. She dropped, exhausted, onto the camp chair at her table and typed out a quick email telling Grant of her discovery. She wanted him to know that his information had paid off, but she wasn't sure what to do with her discovery beyond that. Should she go public and expose Cooper as the fraud he was?

22
CalTech Research Site
Blue Glacier

Saturday, July 9

Kate groaned from the bruising and stiffness from her ordeal the day before as she clomped in snowshoes down to Cooper's Caltech camp. She'd wakened to a clear blue sky and dazzling sunshine. It was ironic given the cloud seeding equipment she'd discovered. She had also decided to confront him with what she'd found, and it gave her pleasure to imagine his surprise.

As she approached the three shelters near the base of Snow Dome, she called out, "Dr. Cooper! Sam!"

Cooper came out of the middle hut wearing a green down vest and a too-broad grin. "Welcome. I was beginning to think you didn't care about our research. Come on in." She removed her snowshoes, and Cooper opened the door, ushering Kate inside.

After she removed her goggles, it took a few seconds for her eyes to adjust to the dim light. She detected the clean but slightly acrid smell of electrical equipment and heard the faint hum of what she assumed were cooling fans. Kate understood why Cooper wore a vest because the room was colder than she would have expected, probably to keep the electronics from overheating. Four racks of instruments lined one side of a plywood walkway leading to two workstations at the far end. At one of them, Sam was hunched over a keyboard wearing earbuds. She got up when she noticed Kate.

"Hi, Dr. Landry." Sam walked over and shook her hand.

"It looks like you do the bulk of your research here in this building," Kate said to Cooper and Sam. "What are in the other two smaller shelters?"

"You might say they're our bedrooms," Sam replied. "I want my privacy."

Cooper pointed with his thumb toward the other end of the shelter. "And I have my own space. We needed a comfortable environment to live in through the winter."

Kate had a grudging respect for what Cooper and Sam must have endured—a personal sacrifice for science. "Tell me about the data you're collecting with this hardware."

Cooper moved closer to her. "I'll take it from here, Sam. You can get back to what you were doing." Sam glared at him before returning to her desk.

Kate looked closely at the first instrument rack that stood about six feet tall and about two feet wide. It held an array of dials, knobs, and switches without any recognizable layout or manufacturer's logo, suggesting to her that it must have been custom made.

Cooper stood with his hand on the side of the rack, like a parent proudly introducing a child. "I've designed and built everything you see here. This first rack contains our weather analysis CPUs." He motioned to the metal tower with flashing LED lights and white gauges with black scale markings. "We've set up remote sensors for monitoring weather conditions throughout Blue Glacier, top to bottom. The raw data is stored on solid-state hard drives for subsequent analysis."

"What exactly are you looking for?" Kate asked.

"We use machine learning algorithms to detect conditions conducive to snow formation prior to, during, and immediately after each storm. I'm building a profile or signature unique to this region telling us why we're getting snow this time of year."

Kate knew this was more of Cooper's bullshit, but she played along. "That's basically what I'm looking for as well."

"That's why I told you we have all the bases covered." He met her eyes and snickered. "You're late to the ballgame."

Kate glared at him. "We'll see." She knew how he'd rigged the game, and she could use that to her advantage.

Cooper clearly enjoyed needling her, smiling while he kept talking. He walked down the row and pointed as he said, "This second rack of instruments is for maneuvering, navigating, and collecting data from our drones. You saw one of them when you first arrived."

"So other than spying on me, what are they good for?" Kate stuck out her chin, thinking of the canister delivery run she'd witnessed.

Cooper didn't take the bait and ignored her. "Among other things, they gather visual evidence of the buildup of snow on the glacier, as it eventually transforms into new glacial ice."

"I hope you're right about the ice formation," she said. "The drones must save you a lot of time and effort hiking all over the mountain."

Sam joined them. "I did *my* share of hiking when we first got here. My job was to install all ten of our remote weather stations from the top to the bottom of Blue Glacier while Cooper stayed here."

Cooper's smile faded. "Someone had to record and calibrate the signals."

"Whatever," Sam said as she returned to her desk.

The tension between the two was unmistakable, which was probably not surprising after spending months cooped up together.

Ignoring Sam, Cooper led Kate to a third instrument rack. "Here I've built the data analysis tools we use to compile, integrate, and display all the data coming from the weather stations."

"Would you characterize that as 'big data' analysis?"

"You could say that. We've collected hundreds of thousands of data points from multiple sources. Let me show you an example." Cooper led Kate to the desk with the three large monitors where he sat and quickly typed several commands on a keyboard. "These graphic images show layers of data from a recent storm. I can display patterns of wind, barometric pressure, and temperature in far greater detail than a typical, single-point weather station."

Kate recognized the faint outline of a topographic map of Mount Olympus and Blue Glacier underlying semitransparent patterns of clouds forming on the left side of the display and moving to the right, presumably west to east. Distinct bands of color came and went, moving and morphing while showing the dynamic changes taking place with incredible resolution.

Cooper continued. "The color and degree of transparency reflect the density and moisture content of the clouds."

The colors and patterns changed as Cooper selected different overlays showing the various weather parameters, like temperature and wind. Six distinct blobs of dark blue surrounded by lighter shades of blue appeared in the clouds over the map above the outline of Mount Tom west of Mount Olympus. They were distributed in such a way that downwind, the entire Blue Glacier was covered by opaque blue, which Cooper said indicated intense snowfall. Kate already knew that the dense snow pattern was his doing and not natural, but Cooper really was capturing authentic weather details. This wasn't just the phony cover story she suspected he'd concocted.

Kate leaned closer to the screen and pointed to the spot where she had discovered the cloud seeding equipment the day before. "This appears to be an area where the most intense snow begins to form."

"You're observant," Cooper said. "Those darker colors are where the topography on the ground intensifies snow production."

Kate knew better. "That's interesting, because I was standing in that very spot yesterday, and there's nothing unusual about the topography. But here's what's unusual." Kate pulled her digital camera from her backpack and brought up one of the photos she'd taken of his cloud seeding generator. "You can spare me the load of crap, Cooper." She pushed the camera in his face.

Sam leapt from her chair and came over to see what was on Kate's camera.

Cooper recoiled and stepped back, his face pale. "What's that thing? Why do you think I have anything to do with it?"

"Don't lie to me. You know it's one of your cloud seeding generators."

"I don't know what you're talking about."

Samantha gawked at the camera, and Kate noticed a flicker of fear in her eyes as she turned to look at her boss.

Kate wasn't about to back down. "You're not here to study the weather. I know you're cloud seeding to enhance snowfall."

Cooper grew quiet and looked at Sam, who stood with her lips pressed tight together. Finally, he said, "Okay. But how'd you find out?"

"I watched your drone deliver this canister." Kate pointed to the upright cylinder in the photo. "What are you trying to prove?"

Cooper paused and then replied. "The technology has been around for seventy years. What's new is studying whether it can reverse the disappearance of glaciers."

Kate lowered her camera. She wasn't expecting such a quick confession, but he seemed sincere. She felt the tension in the room evaporate, and Sam appeared to be breathing again. Kate shifted on her feet. "That's a valid application. But why hide it from everyone? Why pretend the snow buildup is natural?"

Cooper swallowed hard. "If the Park Service knew I'm experimenting with the biggest glacier in the continental US, they'd never have given permission."

"True, but modifying the weather without authorization is illegal. It's also professionally unethical." She crossed her arms across her chest. "How do you expect to publish your results? No journal will touch your research if they know you've enhanced the results."

"Kate, you're missing the big picture here. The weather we're experiencing is historic. Cloud seeding only works if there are clouds to seed. We've had cold air masses and frequent storm fronts that are unprecedented."

She had already thought of this, but his explanation seemed too quick—too prepared. What did he know that he wasn't sharing?

"These are the true side effects of climate change," he said. "The cloud seeding only increases snowfall about ten percent. I'm here to take advantage of this regional weather phenomenon as it increases the mass balance of Blue Glacier."

Kate felt her anger rising again and pointed at him. "I don't like being lied to. And I don't condone your unethical approach to science." She paused. "But I have to admit this buildup of Blue Glacier is a first."

"Exactly. So let's keep on studying." He gave her a broad grin. "Then we can go our separate ways. I don't know of a single alpine glacier that has grown during this age of global warming. Do you? So what if I'm helping it along a little?"

Kate glanced at Sam, who was standing next to the coffee maker with her mug watching them talk. Then she turned back to Cooper. "Your cloud seeding has already contaminated our results. We'd have to deduct the ten percent contributed by the seeding from whatever data we collect. But it might be possible." She figured by conceding something she could learn what else he was up to.

"Good. I was hoping you'd understand. Can I count on you to remain quiet about the cloud seeding until we leave? After that, you can tell whoever you want."

Still annoyed, Kate didn't answer. Still suspicious, she pointed to the fourth rack of instruments. "What's this for?"

Cooper glanced at Sam before answering. "Those instruments are used to monitor weather conditions over the Pacific."

"What conditions?" Kate asked. "That's also one of the regions I'll be studying."

"Oh, mostly cloud density and things like that."

His answer was almost laughably vague, but Kate held her tongue. She knew he was involved in more than he was willing to admit. She looked around the side where the panels didn't cover the components and saw two hefty klystron-type tubes, which were used for high power microwave transmissions, like communicating with satellites. There were also thick coaxial cables running out the back. He was either sending messages worldwide with powerful radio signals or controlling electronic instruments remotely. Maybe he was trying to impress her with his sophisticated equipment without revealing its true purpose.

She turned to face Sam. "You must be very devoted to climate research to be willing to live up here alone all winter with your boss."

Sam glanced at Cooper before answering. "It's been a hard winter, but I'm totally dedicated to understanding and, hopefully, solving global warming." Her answer was bland, almost rehearsed.

"I feel the same way," Kate said. "What have you been working on other than installing the weather stations?"

"In addition to collecting data, my job is to tell the world what's been happening recently on Blue Glacier. You know, social media, press releases. You can find them online yourself, but let me show you a sample." Sam led Kate to her desk.

"Is that a relative?" Kate asked, pointing to a photo on the desk of an older woman standing next to a flower garden.

"My mom. She lives alone in San Jose."

"What does she think about you working on a glacier?"

"She's okay with it, but she'll be glad when we're finished. So will I. Here, let me show you some of my social media posts." Sam sat at her terminal and scrolled through photos highlighting the buildup of snow on one of the sites. Then she ran some dramatic online video footage that the drones had collected of lower Blue Glacier from the air. "It really shows the volume of snow when you look down on it from above."

"I thought I saw on the screen you just showed me that your social media account has almost a million followers. Is that right?"

"Yep." Sam looked up at her with a smug smile.

"Why would so many people care about what's happening on a remote mountaintop like this?"

"It's my job to generate interest. Most of the weather news lately points to global warming. What is happening here on Mount

Olympus is an exception." Sam pointed to the screen showing the thousands of followers. "Lots of people want to know about it."

Yes, and many of them are probably climate-change skeptics, Kate thought. "How do you ensure that your posts aren't being used by the wrong people for the wrong reasons?" The minute she asked the question, Cooper joined them and stared at Sam, as if waiting to hear how she would answer.

"We simply report the facts." Sam shrugged her shoulders but didn't make eye contact with Kate. "We have no control over how people use our information."

Kate tried to cover up her disbelief. Did Sam really say that? As scientists, they had the responsibility to ensure their work wasn't being misused, but did she and Cooper even care? Was empowering the skeptics their goal? Kate gave up trying to get a direct response from either of them. "Well, thank you both for the tour. You have an impressive setup considering you're operating at six thousand feet on top of a glacier."

As she angled toward the door, Cooper pushed in front of her. "Whatever new data you collect this summer will add to the picture we're trying to paint. Glad you came down to visit." He held the door open for her, and she stepped into the cold air.

As Kate clamped on her snowshoes, a voice in her head repeated, "Liar, liar, liar!" She looked sideways and saw a large rectangular metal box with lettering on the side that read "Industrial Generator, 18,000 watts." Cooper and Sam would only need a fraction of that power to receive radio signals and power lights and equipment, so they must be running transmitters with lots of power.

She began climbing back up the side of Snow Dome to her camp, convinced more strongly than ever that the pair's presence on the glacier had a darker purpose than simply documenting a weather anomaly for science. She was determined to find out what they were really up to.

The chilly climb gave her time to reflect on what she'd just seen. She found Cooper's arrogance hard to take, but she couldn't compete head-to-head with his research. He was probably right that she'd just be confirming what he'd already documented. As she snowshoed, she switched her mission. Now all she wanted to do was figure out what he was hiding that meant enough for him to spend the winter on the mountain. Now Dr. Mark Cooper was her subject of inquiry.

23

Caltech Research Site
Blue Glacier

Saturday, July 9

After Kate left their hut, Sam was concerned as she watched Cooper pace up and down the plywood walkway in front of the instrument racks muttering. His being upset didn't come as a complete surprise because Landry always threw him off balance, but she had never seen him this agitated. She knew it was related to the threats the cartel had made to Cooper, and it frightened her.

As she sat at her workstation trying to concentrate on some weather data she was compiling, Cooper's rantings grew louder. "Even if Landry saw our drone, how did she know right where to find the generator?" He didn't wait for an answer, so Sam assumed he wasn't asking her. "She's more dangerous than I thought. If the cartel finds out about Landry, we will *really* have a problem." He kept on like this while walking back and forth for ten minutes.

Finally, when Cooper neared her end of the shelter on one of his circuits, she swiveled in her chair and said, "Why not shut down the operation before Landry discovers more? We've already collected plenty of data showing your geoengineering's effectiveness."

He halted and shook his head. "We can't stop now. I agreed to the cartel's three conditions."

"Which were?"

"First, produce a snowstorm in the middle of July. Second, cause a twenty-degree drop in average temperature for a month. And finally, give them the jet fuel formula. If we don't meet those conditions, we won't get the full payment. And if I don't get enough money to pay for my research to solve global warming, all of our time spent on Blue Glacier will have been wasted."

Sam's anxiety spiked. She rose and stood in Cooper's face. "You're acting like your whole life's at stake here. I don't get it."

Cooper's eyes darted nervously. He didn't seem to be able to look Sam in the eye. "I'm afraid it's true. My life and yours could be at risk."

"What are you talking about?"

Cooper dropped into his desk chair and looked up, wide-eyed. "I was threatened by Faisal, a member of the cartel, who said I'd pay the price if anyone learned of our plan. I assured him our operation was secure. Well, that's not true anymore."

"What did he mean by 'you'd pay the price'?"

"I can only guess, but it's not pretty."

Now Sam began pacing. "I don't like this, Cooper. You're scaring me. I agreed to provide scientific and social media services, but I didn't know about your specific agreement with the cartel to create certain conditions. I certainly wouldn't have joined you knowing there was a threat to our lives." It suddenly hit her that her spying on Cooper may have put both of their lives in danger.

Cooper shrugged. "I thought there was nothing to worry about. I painted all six generators in camouflage and hid them in the trees. There are no roads or trails on that side of the park, so I had each one delivered by helicopter. I never dreamed anyone could find them. Landry apparently walked right up to the nearest one—which is just impossible."

"This is a fucking nightmare! Not only is my career threatened by working for you, but now you're telling me my life's at risk because of your lousy security." She stabbed his chest with her finger. "Well I've had it. I'm leaving." Sam returned to her work station, slammed notebooks shut, and began stacking the photos on her desk.

Cooper stormed over and grabbed her arm. "You can't leave unless I authorize the helicopter to pick you up. And you won't get the last half of your salary if you quit. It's in your contract. And you won't get a single job recommendation from me. If you're smart, you'll keep working another week until we finish."

Sam wrenched away from him and spit out her words. "Cooper, you're a coldhearted SOB." She stomped down the plywood walkway, ripped open the storm flap, and slammed the outer door. After retreating to her personal shelter, she began throwing clothes into her duffel and then collapsed onto her bed. He was right about controlling both her pay and her ability to fly out. If he didn't relent and call for the helicopter, which wasn't likely, she'd have to gut it out for a few more days. After that, she'd decide what direction her career would take—without Cooper, for sure.

Considering how erratic Cooper's behavior was and how obsessed he was with the project, Sam questioned his emotional stability, including his fears that their lives would be in danger if the security breach was discovered. But this time, as Sam sent a report to Tex and the cartel about Kate's visit and discovery of the cloud seeding component of their project, she was deeply conflicted. It gave her more satisfaction than usual to tell them about Cooper's extreme response. Their concerns about the breakdown of Cooper's security arrangements were coming true. At the same time, if the threats Cooper described were true, she could be setting them both up to be killed.

24

Kate Landry's Encampment
Blue Glacier

Saturday, July 9

As she neared her tent, Kate found her mood surprisingly uplifted after her visit to Cooper's compound. She was pleased with herself for confronting him about his cloud seeding. This guy was a sociopath, yet she found herself fascinated by his demeanor.

Back in her tent, Kate made an entry in her scientific journal. She described Cooper's equipment racks and their functions as he told her. Then she summarized her impressions of Cooper, himself, writing that he was capable of designing and building electronic gear and that he had a solid understanding of the underlying dynamics of weather and glacier systems. She wrote that he appeared to be hiding much of what he was up to by not answering her questions or answering them superficially. Something about him bothered her. She added that he had the potential to be dangerous.

She stopped and looked up from her journal. She now had proof that he was actively engaged in weather modification. Not knowing what his reaction would be when she challenged him, Kate was surprised by his forthright admission that he was seeding the clouds to enhance snowfall. Maybe he believed his confident attitude and brazen dismissal of her concerns would reduce their importance, even to her. It was gaslighting, pure and simple. That snake wanted to undermine her self-esteem and make her doubt herself. Rage began to boil, and the way to clear her head was to get outside and focus on her own work. Obsessing about Cooper was a waste of time, and she was sure that once she shook off Cooper's slimy spell, she'd get a new, better perspective.

Out in the brisk air, she climbed the tower that supported the anemometer to record the number of miles of wind that had passed over her camp in the past twenty-four hours. The tower, like the research station, was anchored to bedrock with steel cables, but unlike the research station, which was completely buried under snow and debris, the tower had remained standing as avalanche snow piled up at its base.

Back inside her tent, Kate added the current readings of temperature, humidity, and dew point from her two remote weather stations to a large spreadsheet she was building on her laptop. When she scanned the row of daily readings, she puzzled over why the air temperature had been so stable for the past two and a half weeks, varying daily within a narrow range that was well below normal. There had been no storm fronts since she arrived. Was this a sign that the pattern of strong storms was drawing to an end? Maybe Cooper's cloud seeding would become irrelevant.

That night, as she prepared her modest dinner of dehydrated beef stew and rice, Kate thought maybe she was just lonely. Living on a remote, rugged mountaintop was enough to do that, and she realized this may have been the first time in her life when she was truly alone for more than a few hours. Every summer she had her students with her on the glacier, and at the university, she spent most of her time interacting with students or other faculty members and administrators. The three months she and Grant lived together at the end of the previous summer had been filled with satisfaction. Still, shouldn't a well-adjusted woman be able to live in solitude and function effectively?

She attempted to put those reflections aside so she could sleep. But as she stripped to her long underwear and prepared to crawl into her sleeping bag, she couldn't stop thinking about how her encounter with Cooper had affected her so deeply.

As she began to drift off to sleep, she remembered her dream about feeling helpless in the face of her mother's terminal cancer. As a child, she'd been helpless, but as an adult and a PhD researcher, she was anything but helpless. She considered the impact of having lost her job and being on her own, trying to save the world from climate change. Maybe helpless wasn't the right word, but she was certainly up against huge forces that were far beyond one person to control or overcome.

Suddenly she was wide awake. She couldn't stop stewing, and now her feelings of loss grew to include her entire time on Blue Glacier. For more than eight years, she had tried to understand the dynamics of an alpine glacier that was slowly disappearing due to the warming climate. No matter what she did, she knew that Blue Glacier would one day be just a memory. Maybe someone would mount a commemorative plaque on the side of Mount Olympus just as they had done for the Okjökull Glacier in Iceland. The plaque would read, "Here is the site of the once largest glacier in the lower forty-eight states of America."

Kate felt tears streaming down her cheeks. The loss of this place would be only one of thousands around the world. But this was *her* glacier. This one was special to her. Blue Glacier gave her joy and purpose in life. And it was dying, just as her mother had so many years ago.

It had been steadily dying until that year. Suddenly it was in remission and maybe had a future. Now she realized that Cooper had found a way to enhance the snow and cold on her glacier, giving it a future that it never had before in her lifetime. Maybe Cooper was creating the miracle that she was secretly longing for.

By going back to the glacier, Kate had burned her bridges, so this discovery of Cooper's fraud threw into question the value of the sacrifice she was making. She worried she might be chasing a pipe dream. Yet she was committed to collecting data, even though she knew it was tainted by Cooper's cloud seeding. It alone could not have produced the cold and weather fronts sweeping across the Olympic Peninsula for months. She still needed to learn what else had changed.

Cooper was certainly full of flaws, but she felt a certain respect and even gratitude for what he was trying to do. She knew she should probably report him to some authority for his violation of basic scientific ethics. And she should probably turn him in to the National Park Service for conducting an unauthorized experiment in their national park. But then, so was she, and dammit, she was surprisingly grateful for the results she could see every time she left her tent.

25

Caltech Research Site
Blue Glacier

Sunday, July 10

Cooper rubbed his tired eyes. He'd been staring at his three monitors in the operations hut for an hour monitoring weather over the Pacific. "Eureka!" he shouted. "Here we go. This is what I've been looking for." On the satellite image, he saw the first hint of clouds forming a circular pattern indicating a low pressure system headed toward the Olympic Peninsula.

Every time Cooper enhanced one of these Pacific storms, he knew that he and Sam would be hammered in an ironic twist. The more successful his science, the more miserable their lives would be for a few days. That was the price they had paid all winter with the massive buildup of Blue Glacier they could see all around them.

He barked an order to Sam, who was seated at her workstation across from him. "Power up the microwave transmitter."

Sam scowled but shuffled silently to one of the instrument racks and flipped a couple of switches. The large motor-generator outside dropped in pitch as the high-powered transmitter tubes became active. She returned to her desk without a word.

Cooper's hands flew between the laptop keyboard, mouse, and a custom designed metal box containing switches, knobs, and flashing LED lights. He set in motion a choreographed dance of autonomous boats displayed as red dots on a map on the center monitor of his workstation. These drone boats, unmanned to ensure the secrecy of the operation, had been docked in a secluded cove on the remote west coast of the Olympic Peninsula, waiting for the signal, delivered by satellite, to propel them into the Pacific. Now they charged through the water like a small flotilla of confused battleships spreading out from one another on slightly different headings but in the same general direction from the coast.

Cooper had retrofitted a dozen thirty-foot aluminum-hulled fishing boats with powerful engines, pumps, and tall nozzles of his design to spray a fine mist of seawater high into the base of cloud layers as they formed overhead. He had modelled his design on futuristic vessels proposed in respected scientific publications. The theory predicted that clouds would become thicker and more reflective of sunlight with the addition of seawater mist, thus increasing their tendency to return solar radiation back into space and away from the sea and land below them, lowering the temperature. No one had actually tested this approach to climate control before, but today he would prove it worked.

Each boat cost two million dollars to purchase and retrofit, but he was so confident in his design that he deployed all twelve at once. It had been a major up-front cost for the cartel. At last, he had the chance to show the cartel what he was capable of achieving.

Cooper tapped a key on his laptop and transparent blobs of white overlaid the map, indicating the location of cloud layers from the storm as it approached the coastline, which was also clearly visible as a distinct line on the map. He established target coordinates for each boat by positioning the cursor on the map and clicking. The software and signals sent by satellite told the boats the best location for avoiding collisions with other craft while they pumped up seawater and sprayed it into the sky. With another tap, Cooper's map showed the locations of all ships in the region. Each of his vessels was equipped with radar, so it could detect and move away from any ship that approached within five nautical miles. Cooper then turned a dial on the metal box that signaled the boats to start the pumps and begin spraying.

Once everything was launched, Cooper sat back and observed the red dots moving in predetermined patterns under the clouds. As the sea spray increased the density of the clouds, they turned from misty white to opaque blue on his monitor. He leaned back in his chair and smiled with satisfaction, knowing that his years of creative but diligent research were even more successful than he had hoped. It was unfortunate that his demonstration couldn't be shown to the world because the resulting storm had to appear to be natural.

Cooper thought it was a damn shame his work couldn't be funded by the legitimate science establishments he had approached. He would have been able to publish and be recognized for the contributions he was making. He had been backed into a dark corner of accepting money from the very industry responsible for global warming. At least he would have the satisfaction of knowing his methods worked brilliantly.

Cooper swiveled in his chair and told Sam, "Now we wait. If all goes well and we get the heavy snow I expect, this could be the last storm we need to modify. *Then* we'll be done."

"It can't come soon enough."

"This better work or the cartel won't pay another penny," Cooper added. He couldn't wait to be paid and freed from the threats, and he tried not to think about what might happen if it didn't work. Instead of being paid, he might have to pay with his life.

He checked in periodically all morning, watching the blue color spread and the cloud boundaries slowly merge and approach their position on the Olympic Peninsula. Since the boats were designed to operate autonomously. There wasn't much for him to do but wait for the storm to arrive, so he left for his own shelter.

Later that afternoon, Sam called to Cooper through his door. "Coop, your storm has arrived. The weather station indicates the wind on Mount Olympus is already gusting above thirty knots."

He opened the door, nodded at Sam, and looked up at the clouds moving swiftly overhead. "Beautiful. This should make Landry's life miserable in her flimsy tent."

26

Kate Landry's Encampment
Blue Glacier

Sunday, July 10

The sun turned the bright nylon fabric a flaming red as it lit up the east wall of Kate's tent. She yawned, climbed out of her sleeping bag, and pulled on a heavy sweater and pants over the long underwear she'd slept in. Before doing anything else, she counted her remaining food supplies. There were ten ramen meals, four packs of beef jerky, and six packets of instant oatmeal. She *had* to solve the puzzle of the bizarre weather—soon.

Analysis of weather data from her instruments and online sources provided her with a baseline for evaluating the day-to-day changes and, in some cases, the hour-by-hour transitions. She needed to stay attuned to these trends to detect any events that fell outside of the average ranges she'd recorded. But nothing significant had occurred in the weather since she first flew to Blue Glacier. In fact, the weather had been surprisingly sunny and calm.

As Kate finished her breakfast, she made her daily check of the real-time imagery of cloud formation over the Pacific from NOAA's satellite feeds on the internet. She nearly choked on her last mouthful of oatmeal when she saw a striking and unusual pattern. Instead of the typical band of uniform, light-colored clouds in the black-and-white satellite pictures, she detected a distinct pattern superimposed on the light gray background. She'd never seen anything like it. She counted twelve distinct cloud shapes in a formation over the Pacific and upwind of the Olympic Peninsula, nearly equally spaced, where thick clouds formed in a geometrical pattern. Not a natural occurrence, she was sure.

As she watched, the clouds grew opaque, which indicated higher density, as ever-widening triangles formed downwind from each point source. She was struck by it. This was similar to the pattern she had seen on Cooper's display that had confirmed his cloud seeding operation. The difference was that the point sources for cloud seeding remained fixed while the points over the ocean seemed to move in tight circles. Her spine tingled with the excitement of this discovery.

Could the storms hammering the Olympics all year have resulted from the cloud thickening she was seeing on the satellite imagery? Could these clouds supply Cooper's seeding operation with the moisture needed to produce the enhanced snowfall? As Cooper himself had pointed out, cloud seeding was an established technology used in one form or another since the end of World War II, but she'd never heard of a technology to thicken clouds over the ocean like she was observing.

Kate took a video screenshot of the moving patterns and saved it to her computer's online storage. She wanted to send Grant an email with a link to the video to see if his NCAR associates could identify what the patterns might mean, but she hesitated before typing, trying to decide how to start. "Good morning!" was too perky. She decided to just begin as she would with anyone else and typed "Grant" with a comma after it and stuck to the facts. She added a quick "Thanks for your help" at the end and hit "send." Better to keep it all very professional.

After seeing what the resulting clouds and storm produced, she'd have more information to share. Then she could be more personable that night during their video call. She was grateful that Grant was willing to help her from a distance—geographically *and* emotionally.

That afternoon, Kate looked toward the Pacific and saw signs of the approaching storm: high cirrus clouds overhead with a dark stratus layer on the horizon. The weather radar display on her laptop confirmed this would be one of those intense weather events she'd heard had impacted the Olympic Peninsula every few days all year. The circular shape and barometric pressure gradient revealed a bomb cyclone, an unusually intense storm characterized by a sudden and significant drop in atmospheric pressure. She was in the bullseye of this major system approaching from the Pacific. Would her tent hold up in the face of such fury?

She didn't have a lot of time before she'd be hit with the strongest wind she'd ever experienced while working on the glacier. Scrambling around to be sure everything was tight and secure, she tugged on the nylon cords anchoring her tent to the snow. She even piled snow around the west-facing wall and packed it down to form a windbreak. When she looked up at the ridge crest above her tent, she saw the spinning cups on the anemometer telling her the wind was picking up, although she already felt it on her face. The readout on her laptop from the two remote weather stations confirmed the wind speed was twenty-five knots on the lower glacier and thirty-five on Panic Peak above her location.

What got her attention wasn't the wind speed but the barometric pressure dropping so quickly. She felt her chest tighten when she saw online that the barometric pressure from ships to the west registered a fall of more than one hundred millibars—the conditions that defined a bomb cyclone. Kate would have been worried if she'd had to ride out such a storm in the UW research station anchored to bedrock. But the thought of being in a tent anchored to snow with flimsy nylon cords made her hands shake and her neck muscles tighten.

Right on schedule at seven that evening, Kate initiated a video call to Grant. This time she hoped to see his face in real time—if her internet connection was strong enough. With the click of her mouse, Grant's sober face filled her laptop screen. She was disappointed. Was he going to be all business as he'd been on their last call? Then she reminded herself she'd been all business too.

"How was your day in the land of snow and ice?" he asked. But before she could answer, he went on. "Here, let me show you what I'm looking at from the NCAR library." He turned his laptop around to show her his view out the window that opened to the hillside with its forest and grasslands below and to the south of the lab. Late afternoon cumulus clouds on the horizon glowed orange in the low sun and a half dozen wind turbines turned lazily on the distant mesa. "Can you believe this view?"

At least he was being personable, but was he choosing this moment to make a sales pitch for Boulder? She offered a weak smile and replied, "That's really pretty. But listen, I'm about to get slammed by one monster of a storm. Did you get my email with the link to the video in my cloud storage?"

She noticed Grant's jaw tightening. "Yes, you're right. The video looked strange."

"I suspect Cooper is responsible somehow, and I'm thinking of contacting the Coast Guard to see if they can locate boats under the spots."

"I wouldn't do that, Kate. We don't know if it's human caused and we certainly don't know if Cooper was behind it. I'll ask Liu to see if she can tell us what the spots on the video you sent me might mean. Then go from there."

"But it might be too late if we wait."

"If you call the Coast Guard, it might reveal you're not with the university anymore. You've got to slow down."

She felt hot blood rushing to her face but realized he was right. "I'll wait, but please find out what Liu thinks and get back to me as soon as you can tomorrow, okay?"

He cleared his throat, which he usually did when he was irritated with something, and said, "I'm trying to help you, but do whatever you want."

Kate realized she'd come on stronger than she intended. "I'm sorry, Grant. This storm has got me nervous, and I'm almost out of the meals I brought. I need to know what's causing the bizarre weather, and I don't have much time. Let's talk again tomorrow."

"Okay," he replied. "I'm concerned about you, so *do* contact me tomorrow to let me know you're safe. Okay?"

She nodded and then closed the session. She felt edgy and impatient, but her impatience was quickly overshadowed by worry. Her immediate concern was surviving the storm bearing down on her.

Harsh blasts of freezing wind began hammering Kate's tent as she crawled into her sleeping bag, fully dressed. Lying on her cot, she felt surprisingly warm and safe with a storm raging outside, but her heart skipped a beat every time she felt the tent shudder from a gust smacking it. The abrupt snapping of the nylon fabric in and out with each blast made it impossible for her to sleep. When particularly strong gusts began buffeting the tent, Kate got up to check the anemometer readout from the summit of Panic Peak, and what she saw took her breath away. Gusts were topping ninety-three miles an hour—hurricane force. How foolish to think she would be safe even in a rugged five-season tent in weather like this.

Since she had erected her tent on snow and not solid ground, she'd buried large rocks under two feet of snow to serve as anchors for the six nylon stays. With gusts hitting every few seconds, would the cords come loose, causing the whole structure to collapse on her?

27

Kate Landry's Encampment
Blue Glacier

Monday, July 11

The storm dragged on hour after hour, and at about one in the morning she got up and put on her down parka and climbing boots. Holding the most powerful flashlight she had, she stumbled out and was hit in the face by a blast of icy wind and stinging snowflakes. She could barely breathe. Never in eight previous summers had it ever gotten this cold. She was forced to crawl on her hands and knees because standing upright was impossible in the gale.

She struggled around the tent, inspecting the stays. A large drift had formed on the south side, completely burying the generator. Fortunately, she'd had the forethought to use only battery power during the storm. Otherwise, the snow might have shorted out or otherwise ruined the generator if she'd left it running.

One of the cords had come loose on the west wall. The fabric whipped in the wind, and the tent nearly collapsed at that spot. She crawled back into the tent and dragged out a shovel to dig up the rock anchor. To retie the line, she had to take off her gloves, but her stiff fingers barely worked. Finally, she buried the rock and stood awkwardly against the wind to pack the snow down with her boots. After crawling back inside, she lay on the floor, shaking in spite of her parka and layers of clothes. The tip of her nose and her earlobes were numb, and when she checked using a small mirror, they were white, indicating frostbite. She tried to thaw them out using her bare hands.

At about two in the morning, her remote weather instruments indicated the wind had shifted from southwest to southeast, which meant the most intense part of the storm had passed further inland. She relaxed a little, but fatigue and the nonstop clamor of the tent fabric flapping in and out had left her drained. Just when the worst seemed to be over, a roaring blast hammered the tent, snapping one of the aluminum tent poles.

Kate's nightmare was coming true. She couldn't stand up, and the weight of the snow on the top of the tent pushed her to the floor. The tent fluttered around the edges. Would it get blasted loose from all its anchors and somersault down the mountain? All she could do was lie flat, letting the fabric rest on top of her and hope that her weight plus that of her bed, desk, and equipment would be enough to hold it down. She would have to wait in the damaged tent until the wind died down enough for her to try to make repairs.

By five she could wait no longer. She had to use the privy, which she'd erected where the old generator shed and outhouse had once stood. When she opened her tent flap, the new snow was close to three feet deep, and the wind had blown drifts significantly higher. She needed snowshoes and ski poles even to travel the short distance. At least the wind was less intense, so she could walk close to upright. The small tent she'd erected for privacy had blown completely away, and she felt exposed and a little silly sitting on the toilet out in the open, even though there wasn't anyone around for miles to see her in this condition. Still, she could barely wait to get up from the ice-cold seat.

On the way back to the damaged tent, struggling through the powder, she realized she wouldn't be going far that day. Once back inside, she pushed up on the tent roof to get the heavy snow to slide off and then lashed one of her ski poles to the broken tent post as a sort of splint. It would have to do until she could make more permanent repairs.

Meanwhile, she'd stay inside and keep working. She could analyze data from her remote weather stations and the weather sites available on the internet. First, she had to dig out the generator from the drift burying it. The tripod holding the dish antenna had blown over and had to be propped back up and repositioned to align with the antenna on Hurricane Ridge. It took a half hour of tweaking the dish orientation while watching the display on her laptop to lock in the strongest signal possible. At last, it worked.

To focus her concentration, Kate wrote some notes in her journal. "What are the specific conditions to produce snow on the glacier in July? (Theoretical answer is supercooled liquid water plus 'seeds' such as dust particles or Cooper's cloud seeding that create a nucleus for each snowflake to form.) But how did the moisture in these clouds become supercooled?"

She got to work researching the answer to her own question. Weather reports from surrounding communities indicated there had been light precipitation to the north of her in Port Angeles, mostly in the form of rain mixed with snow. But Victoria, twenty-five miles farther north, was overcast with no precipitation. She checked the weather to the south and learned that Olympia had, like Victoria, experienced clouds, but there had been no precipitation. The cloud buildup must have been associated with the pattern of thickening she had observed, while the precipitation had been enhanced by Cooper's cloud seeding, squeezing moisture from the clouds.

Since the storm seemed less intense, Kate checked the satellite feed to see if the weather was clearing to the west. Her shoulders slumped when she saw the band of clouds off the Olympic Peninsula was still there, meaning even more snow was on the way. The point-source thickening of clouds was still evident too, but it appeared to be fading.

Even as she watched, the clouds moving toward the coast were beginning to break up and thin. Two of the cloud thickening spots had already become so faint they were barely visible on the screen. There *had* to be boats of some kind under each of the spots, and Cooper was involved. She felt that tingle along her spine that told her she was on to something. She couldn't wait for the next wave of storms because she'd be out of food and forced to leave the glacier before then. This was her last chance, and she couldn't wait to hear back from Grant. She had to get someone to investigate these spots before the clouds dissipated completely and the unusual patterns were no longer detectable.

She typed in a search for the Seattle Coast Guard's phone number and punched it in on her internet-connected cell phone. When a man she assumed was a sailor answered, she said, "I'm Dr. Kate Landry calling from the Blue Glacier Project on Mount Olympus. I have an urgent request and need to speak with the commander in charge."

"What is the nature of your request?"

She wanted to make her case and expected to be questioned, so she forced herself to be polite. "I have evidence of unauthorized weather modification in the Pacific, west of the Olympic Peninsula. It's resulted in violent weather that has contributed to civilian deaths." She hoped her account sounded serious enough.

He put Kate on hold, and her fingers drummed on the edge of her laptop while she waited. She waited and waited some more. When she checked her internet connection, the signal strength had dropped too low to support her phone call. She blurted out, "Fuck!"—a word she rarely used. After five minutes, the internet signal recovered and she requested to be connected to the commander once more.

"This is Rear Admiral Jesse Lopez. How can I help you?"

She tried not to sound too eager or impatient, just scientific. "Sir, I've detected an unusual pattern of high density clouds that have formed to the west of the Olympic Peninsula. These clouds are moving inland and producing a rare snowstorm in July where I'm camped about a thousand feet below the summit of Mount Olympus."

She could almost hear him shrug over the phone.

"Why is this so urgent? It's not unusual for the Olympics to receive snow in the summer."

"I'm aware of that, sir, but as we speak, I'm looking at a satellite image of an unusual pattern of clouds that appear to be created and enhanced artificially by a fleet of boats of some kind. I'm calling to see if you can help. If you send a Coast Guard vessel to the coordinates of one of these high density cloud spots, we can verify that they are human caused. Such an unauthorized weather modification would be illegal, would it not?"

"Send me an email with the coordinates closest to the coast." Admiral Lopez gave her the address to use. "But Dr. Landry, it would be a violation of Coast Guard policy for us to conduct a potentially hazardous mission at sea without a confirmed threat. You've described what might turn out to be a naturally occurring anomaly. Although it might represent illegal activity, there doesn't appear to be a direct threat."

"But sir, couldn't you divert one of your cutters that are already conducting a mission?"

"I understand what you're asking, Dr. Landry, but it would be against Coast Guard policy to assign this to a regularly scheduled mission. I'm sorry."

After ending the call, Kate hung her head, feeling a mixture of frustration and embarrassment. She desperately wanted to confirm her theory about the cloud pattern, but she was dependent on outside help to investigate and confirm it. How foolish and naïve to assume she could convince the Coast Guard to get involved. On top of that, she had gone against Grant's advice and acted impulsively. Still, desperate times called for desperate measures. She at least made the attempt.

28

Caltech Research Site
Blue Glacier

Monday, July 11

An alarm sounded and a light on the instrument rack flashed a piercing red light. Cooper leapt up from his workstation and ran to check it and turn it off.

"Jesus, what was that?" Sam called out, swiveling in her chair to watch him.

The light and alarm could only mean one thing: A ship of some kind had come within the five-mile perimeter of one of Cooper's drone boats. "Incursion alarm on boat number seven," he replied. "Bring up the radar display for that boat."

After a minute of clicking keys on her terminal, Sam said, "It's up. Sent it to your display."

Cooper returned to his desk and stared at the radar display as it swept a full circle every few seconds. A bright dot appeared in the upper right quadrant and moved steadily toward the center where his drone boat was located. "Give me a visual," he barked.

"Coming your way." Sam typed commands on her keyboard, and the image of a ship appeared on her screen, which was mirrored on the right-hand monitor on Cooper's desk.

"It's a damn Coast Guard cutter," he yelled. "You can tell by the red stripe near the bow. The radar display indicates it's a little over four miles away and headed straight toward my boat. Let's get away from it." He flipped a switch. "The evasion routine will start in a minute."

As soon as the cutter crossed the four-mile circle on the radar display, the image of the ship from the video camera began to shake and grow smaller as Cooper's boat started its engine and sped away at full throttle.

Cooper stayed glued to the radar image for a minute before exhaling. He watched the boat image move away, putting distance between it and the cutter, but the Coast Guard followed, responding to the evasive maneuvers. "Shit! They're in pursuit." He slammed his hand on the desk. "Someone must have tipped them off. They *really* want to intercept us!"

"Wait. It looks like they've stopped," Sam said.

On the radar display, Cooper saw that the cutter's echo had stopped moving. "Yeah, but now they've launched two smaller boats," Cooper said as two dots of light departed the cutter's echo, headed toward the drone at the center of the display. "They're faster, more maneuverable—probably Zodiacs." He winced in frustration. "Damn! We won't be able to outrun them."

Within five minutes, the smaller crafts had closed the distance to the drone boat, with one approaching from each side. "We can't let them board." Cooper stood and began pacing, checking his monitor every few seconds. "Even though there's no crew for them to interrogate, my equipment is too valuable to fall into the government's hands."

As the two boats approached within a hundred yards, Cooper returned to the instrument rack and flipped open the red safety cover over a toggle switch. "Here goes nothing." He flipped the switch. The rumble from the large motor generator outside their shelter dropped in pitch as the load from the large transmitter tubes increased. He watched as the radar and video screens went blank.

"What did you *do*?" Sam shouted.

He glanced over to see her sitting with an open mouth. "I just scuttled two million dollars' worth of boat." Cooper pounded his desk with his fist. "What a waste! Did you see how the Coast Guard chased it?" He began pacing. "Someone told them about our boats, and there's only one person I can think of who might have figured it out."

"Dr. Landry."

"Right." Cooper's face turned scarlet. "She's too smart for her own good."

29

Kate Landry's Encampment
Blue Glacier

Monday, July 11 and Tuesday, July 12

"I just survived the worst storm of my life," Kate said to Grant that evening on their video call. The fabric of her tent wall snapped back and forth like a loose sailboat mainsail in the diminishing winds. She could see her breath and was bundled in her parka and insulated pants.

"Are you okay?" Grant asked. "You look cold."

"I'm fine, but we got about three feet of new snow and the temperature dropped below freezing. Our wind speeds topped ninety-five miles an hour, well above hurricane force. After an especially strong blast hit my tent, it collapsed, and I've had to make temporary repairs." She gave him a brief summary of the previous night. "After the storm passed, I called the Coast Guard base in Seattle because the cloud pattern I showed you was fading. I was afraid I might not see those spots again." She sighed. "And I can't stay here much longer without a way to get food."

"What did the Coast Guard say?"

"I talked to the commander in charge, and he told me they wouldn't send a ship to investigate. They needed more information to go on. I guess my word wasn't enough."

"I told you to wait until I could get back to you." Grant shook his head, and his voice had an edge to it. "After we talked, I showed Dr. Liu the video of your screenshots. She was intrigued by the spots but not sure what they were. So she contacted a meteorologist at the Boulder office of NOAA, and together they analyzed the movement of the point sources in the satellite images. They determined the spots moved in well-defined circles, maintaining fixed distances between them. They were sure it wasn't a natural pattern but one set in motion by humans."

"Thanks for doing that. Now I have a stronger case for going back to the Coast Guard."

Grant frowned and shook his head. "I wish you'd waited. That won't work now. Things have gotten more complicated."

"Complicated how?"

"Liu and her contact at NOAA made inquiries through their government connections and found that you've uncovered evidence of an unauthorized weather intervention. This is a violation of international law and poses a threat because it could potentially be weaponized. People are worried about China or some other country using weather modification destructively."

"We're on the same wavelength. That's what I said to Rear Admiral Lopez with the Coast Guard, and it didn't change his mind. He was all about following protocol."

"Liu and her fellow scientist at NOAA said they had an obligation to notify Homeland Security."

Kate groaned. "Oh, great. You warned me. Once the authorities get involved, we'll lose control over our own research." Kate pounded her table with her fist. "We may never learn what made the clouds thicken and Cooper's involvement, if any."

"You can only do so much up there on your own," Grant said. "It's time to let the authorities take over."

"I'm going to get to the bottom of what's happening up here. Now I've got work to do."

"I hope you can, and you're right," he replied. "I'm here if you need any more help with your data."

"Thanks, Grant. I actually do appreciate all you've done."

When they ended the call, Kate was torn. She wanted Grant's approval, but she was determined to keep going with or without it. Now, more than ever, she wanted to get to the bottom of whatever Cooper was up to. She needed to keep studying. While she worked on her laptop, the steady purring of the motor generator outside her tent, along with the rhythm of the flapping tent fabric in the wind, provided a steady beat. Her suspicions about the cloud pattern had proven correct, so now the missing piece was whatever it was Cooper had done to lower the air temperature enough to produce snow when rain was the norm at this time of year.

The wind growled with increased menace, startling Kate. A thought dawned on her. Cooper would probably be arrested for his illegal geoengineering activities. The idea of a scientist getting thrown in jail for doing his work was disturbing. She thought of Galileo, imprisoned for saying Earth wasn't the center of the universe. But Cooper was different. He seemed to have gone rogue instead of working in cooperation with legitimate scientific entities. If his science was sound, why go it alone? Probably his ego was too big to share the spotlight. There was a lot she didn't know. But how dangerous might he become to keep from being caught?

―――

Early the following morning, a mysterious email arrived in Kate's inbox from the public affairs office of the Thirteenth Coast Guard District. It contained a press release from the US Coast Guard stating, "The crew of the Coast Guard Cutter *Intrepid* returned home Monday following a diversion from its planned course to identify a vessel suspected of operating illegally off the coast of the Olympic Peninsula. The crew interdicted the vessel at the coordinates provided by an anonymous source."

Kate had to stop reading. She couldn't breathe. The anonymous source must have been her, which meant she needed to be careful because she didn't like to think what Cooper might do if he found out. She prepared some instant oatmeal and kept reading her screen.

The press release reported that the vessel was spraying sea water into the clouds overhead in what appeared to be a form of weather modification, and when the sailors attempted to stop the vessel, it sped away and then sank after an explosion. No crew members were observed before or after the sinking. The vessel appeared to be operating autonomously. The press release said that both Homeland Security and the local field office of the FBI had been notified.

Kate was shaken to the core by the time she finished reading. If that boat was part of Cooper's operation, he was more dangerous than she had suspected, and so far, all the evidence pointed in that direction. As she contemplated that fact, she slowly stretched her neck, which was nearly frozen from the accumulated stress of the last few days.

Had anyone been on board the vessel that sank? She hoped the boats were piloted remotely, just like Cooper's drones. But if the Zodiac had reached the boat as it sank, Coast Guard sailors could have died. "My God, Cooper, you're capable of murder," Kate said out loud.

Kate decided to call her Coast Guard contact, Rear Admiral Lopez, to see if he could fill her in. She retrieved the number she'd called the previous day, and the sailor who answered seemed to recognize her name and connected her to the commander. "Rear Admiral, this is Dr. Kate Landry. I read a news release just now detailing an encounter between one of your cutters and a vessel that was spraying seawater into the clouds."

"Yes, Dr. Landry. I asked that you be sent a copy of the release. I'm afraid that's all I'm free to disclose since this is an ongoing criminal investigation. The press release included details we would normally not disclose, but our intent was to prompt the owners of the boat to respond so we can identify who they are."

"I thought you said it was against your policy to divert a mission, but the news release said that's exactly what happened." She felt annoyed that he had said one thing to her but then done the opposite.

"I can tell you that after you and I talked, we received orders from Homeland Security to investigate the vessel."

Aha! The admiral was ordered to check it out. "Thank you for sharing your information. It confirms my suspicion that some kind of geoengineering was underway."

"I'm afraid you're correct, but we weren't allowed to respond to your request as a private citizen. We have to follow protocol."

"Now that you've confirmed the illegal activity, you should know I have information about what I believe was the mission of the boat that exploded and the person no doubt responsible." She thought now he'd want to hear what she had to say.

"Dr. Landry, that would be helpful, I'm sure, but the investigation has been turned over to the FBI. You need to call the Seattle Field Office and ask for agent Jasmine Sasani. Thanks for your help, and good luck."

Kate terminated the call and texted Grant. "New information. Check your email. We'll talk later." The news release that she forwarded to him would speak for itself.

30

Caltech Research Site
Blue Glacier

Tuesday, July 12

Sam discovered the press release from the Coast Guard through her daily keyword search of weather news related to the Olympic Peninsula and showed it to Cooper. "Here's the Coast Guard's account of what happened Monday. As you suspected, someone tipped them off."

She braced herself for an explosion as soon as Cooper began to read. She could sense his growing rage as his face grew deeper and deeper red. He was getting out of control. Could his anger lead to violence? She was beginning to worry that it might.

"Landry had to have been the source," he yelled, exploding. "She could have seen the pattern of cloud thickening on a public satellite feed and reported the locations of the thickest spots to the Coast Guard." He slammed a book on his desk with such force that papers and pens flew onto the floor. "Why can't we do anything to modify the weather without that nosy woman discovering it? This is worse than ever because she reported it to the authorities."

Sam felt her body tense up, so she stood and paced to unwind. "Well, it explains why the cutter seemed so determined to chase down your boat. You'd better hope the cartel doesn't find out about this."

"They have ways of monitoring our work that you and I don't know," Cooper said in what was almost a whisper.

Sam looked down to avoid eye contact, hoping he didn't suspect *her*. She had to be careful. When she looked up, Cooper was staring at her with a quizzical expression.

Suddenly, Landry's voice came through the handheld transceiver on the back of Cooper's workstation. "Cooper, are you there?"

He flinched, and his face went pale.

"Hello. This is Dr. Landry. Does this thing still work?" Her voice sounded far away on the small radio. Sam realized the transceiver had gone unused since Landry called for help after the avalanche.

Sam smirked at Cooper's startled response. He was perfectly okay spying on *her* from his drone, but he was freaking out when *she* turned up unannounced. The radio, intended as a lifeline, had now become threating to Cooper.

He snatched up the transceiver. "Cooper here. What's wrong?"

"Nothing's wrong. Just wanted to see how you and Sam weathered our latest storm." Landry's conversational tone surprised Sam. It was not what she expected from someone who'd just experienced a bomb cyclone in a tent. Sam's admiration of Kate's tough character grew even more.

Cooper squinted at Sam and shook his head. "That was an average storm for us. We had much worse last winter. But how'd you make out in your tent?" The sneer on his face revealed the pleasure he'd taken in making her life miserable.

"I had some damage and had to make some minor repairs, but otherwise, no problem."

Sam knew it had to have been hell. Was she putting a positive spin on it just to give Cooper a hard time?

"I'm curious. Did you do your cloud seeding?" Kate asked.

"I always do when the conditions are right."

"You do anything else to enhance the storm's intensity?"

She was obviously fishing. If Dr. Landry had called the Coast Guard, she knew the answer.

"Like what?" His voice grew louder. "If you're accusing me of something, spit it out."

"I know your boats have been thickening the clouds, and I know that moisture should be falling as rain, not snow. What have you done to lower the temperature?"

Cooper grinned broadly. "I'm flattered that you give me so much credit." Then the grin quickly faded to a frown. "But I thought you were a better scientist than this. Haven't you read how the jet stream has been behaving erratically? Every time it drops this far south, it draws arctic air with it. These temperature anomalies are the result." He looked to Sam, obviously looking for her to be impressed with his brilliant comeback.

Instead, Sam stared at him in disbelief. Kate could easily disconfirm his phony explanation. His response sounded defensive, as if Kate had touched a nerve. Which she had. Sam shook her head and made a throat-cutting gesture with her index finger. If he wasn't more careful, Kate might uncover his entire weather modification scheme. She'd already found out most of it. His crude lies were so inept that he risked getting them both in trouble with the cartel.

Sounding genuinely relaxed, Kate replied, "Take it easy, Cooper. I've just never experienced a storm like this in all the time I've been coming up here. I thought you might have had something to do with it."

When Cooper didn't respond, Kate added, "I guess not. Well, I'm glad to hear you two are okay. I'll keep documenting this weather until I leave."

Now the conversation was getting interesting. "When will that be?" he asked, leaning forward in his chair.

"I haven't decided yet."

Cooper slumped as she evaded the question and said, "Sam and I won't be staying here much longer. About another week."

That was news to Sam. It annoyed her that he'd just told Kate before bothering to let her know.

Maintaining her casual tone, Kate replied, "Oh, really? I'll probably be going about then too."

Sam stared at her boss wondering why she'd ever agreed to come work for him in the first place. They both shared the same goal of reversing global warming. But so did Kate, and she had far more conviction and character. If only Kate had offered her the job instead of Cooper, she would have taken it in a heartbeat.

Sam made the excuse to Cooper that she wasn't feeling well, which she wasn't, so she could go to her personal shelter and send Tex a message. He needed to know that Kate had notified the Coast Guard and that Cooper was pissed off. Had the cartel come across the Coast Guard's news release? If so, they needed to know how unstable Cooper was becoming. In this state he might do something stupid and dangerous.

31

Kate Landry's Encampment
Blue Glacier

Tuesday, July 12

Kate examined the flimsy ski-pole splint that kept her tent aloft. She doubted it would hold up against another storm, and she'd have to leave Blue Glacier soon anyway—perhaps for the last time. Now that Cooper would be departing in a week, his weather modification would soon stop. She had discovered the cloud seeding and marine cloud enhancement, but no natural changes could account for the temperature drop. So how had Cooper cooled the atmosphere enough to make it snow? The rest of her time on the glacier needed to be focused on answering that question.

Kate scanned the internet looking for clues and found several. During the most recent storm, the jet stream tracked farther north, not south as Cooper claimed. This would have produced warmer air temperatures rather than cooler. But moored buoy data in NOAA's World Ocean Database showed lower than normal ocean and air temperatures extending several hundred miles west of her location on the Olympic Peninsula.

Another clue came from Washington State's air monitoring network, which showed a spike in sulfur dioxide during the same time the temperatures along the Washington coast fell below normal. This hinted that a form of geoengineering that had been proposed to cool the planet might have been deployed. It involved injecting sulfur dioxide particles into the atmosphere to mimic what happened when volcanic eruptions caused cooling for months or years.

Kate's eyes were burning from staring for hours at her screen and rebooting each time her internet connection dropped out. She stood up and stretched. Then she heated water to add to one of her three remaining dehydrated meals. The research she'd been poring over all day caromed around in her brain as she waited for the flakes to become edible food. When ash and sulfur particles spewed from volcanoes, the atmosphere cooled for months after the eruption. If you could replicate the effects of a volcano through geoengineering, could you slow or halt atmospheric and surface warming? Yes, theoretically, but how might you do that practically?

She picked up her mug of tea, walked to the flap of her tent, and looked out toward the Pacific. A crisscrossing patchwork of jet contrails fanned out from the Seattle area and lit up an otherwise cloudless blue sky. Suddenly an idea hit her. What if all the commercial jets flying to Asia from the Seattle-Tacoma airport were somehow being used to modify the weather?

She hurried back to her laptop and quickly found a number of conspiracy theories that had been posted online accusing the government of secretly dispersing chemicals using aircraft. In fact, they'd invented the term "chemtrails" to describe the long, narrow clouds created by passing aircraft high in the atmosphere. Normally, contrails were formed from condensing water vapor. But how could sulfur particles be dispersed on a large enough scale without someone detecting it?

Kate checked her internet connection speed and found it was fast enough to allow her to make at least a brief cell phone call.

She pulled up the number of Tyrone, a retired airline pilot friend she knew in her condo building in Seattle.

When he answered and she identified herself, he said, "I haven't seen you for a while."

"I moved out temporarily. I'm actually calling you from Blue Glacier on the side of Mount Olympus. I've got a question for you."

"I've never talked to someone on a mountaintop before. What's up?"

"This is a strange question, but is it possible for sulfur to be added to jet fuel to produce sulfur dioxide in the exhaust?"

"Sounds like you've been reading those conspiracy theories about chemtrails."

"Yes, I've read them, but this is a serious question. I have a theory, but not a conspiracy theory. Is it possible to burn sulfur in jet fuel?"

"I suppose so, but it's not likely. Airports screen the sulfur content of fuel they deliver to their jets because burning sulfur produces sulfur oxides, which engines don't like. It damages nickel alloy engine components and results in frequent and costly repairs. They do everything possible to eliminate sulfur."

"Sounds like the answer is no." She felt her spine sag, as if the air had been let out of her lungs. Feeling completely deflated, she made pleasant conversation to be polite. When they came to a natural pause in the conversation, she thanked him and hung up.

Though Tyrone's answer was disappointing, she couldn't let go of the idea of sulfur entering the atmosphere via airplanes. He didn't say it wouldn't work, just that safeguards would have to be overcome. But how could anyone bypass the screening for an entire airport that hosted numerous airline companies?

Kate didn't have time to waste wallowing in feeling discouraged and raising doubts. She decided to confirm the scientific basis for her theory and emailed Grant to ask Dr. Liu whether commercial jets disbursing sulfur dioxide particles could cool the atmosphere.

After a half hour, Grant replied with information from Liu. Sulfur dioxide injected into the atmosphere at the altitudes that commercial jetliners flew would be dissipated and fall too quickly to affect the climate. Most of the modeling Liu had done of possible solar radiation management assumed that the sulfur was injected higher up into the stratosphere, where it would linger for weeks before dissipating.

It was another disappointing response to her idea, yet she had a strong sense she was right. She typed her reasoning back to Grant. "Think of all the aircraft in all the airlines flying between the West Coast and Asia every day. Would that not replenish the sulfur dioxide on a daily basis, even if it falls out quickly? Do you remember when all commercial flights were grounded for days after 9/11? It made a detectable difference on temperatures measured on the ground. So jet exhaust can affect ground temperature."

In his final email, Grant admitted it was possible but said it was an empirical question that would have to be tested in the field running numbers with the volume of fuel.

So it would be up to her to answer the question. She researched how many scheduled flights departed Sea-Tac flying west every day and how many tons of fuel each flight burned. Then she calculated the amount of exhaust disbursed into the atmosphere. All the data reinforced her suspicion that Cooper's third form of geoengineering *could* be coming from burning jet fuel laced with sulfur. But how did he get his fuel past airport screening?

32

Caltech Research Site
Blue Glacier

Wednesday, July 13

Early evening, when the sun was already on the west side of Snow Dome and the encampment was in shadow, Cooper flipped the circuit breaker, stopping the noisy generator and powering all the instruments in the operations hut using battery power. They often did this to savor the incredible quiet that permeated life on the glacier.

He planned to nail down the final report for the cartel and dazzle them with how he had met and exceeded their objectives. He felt an urgency to finish this and was anxious for them to wire the remainder of the money owed him before they got news of the security breach. How was it possible that despite his efforts to keep it hidden, Kate had uncovered two of his three geoengineering components in such a short time? Now he regretted she wasn't killed in his first avalanche.

Sam sat at her workstation across from Cooper. She had been updating all the tables and charts of data they had been collecting since January and had worked nonstop since the night before. She hadn't bothered to change clothes and barely took time to eat. She seemed as eager to finish and leave as he was, but he kept nudging her along anyway.

"Be sure to include the most recent storm figures," Cooper said. "We need to showcase how I made it snow in the summer."

She stood abruptly and turned toward him. "Stop micromanaging me! I always incorporate the latest data in my charts. If you want me to finish, just leave me alone."

Cooper jabbed his index finger into the air. "We've got one shot at this."

"The data speaks for itself. It snowed in July in the Olympics while it's hotter than hell in the rest of the United States. If that doesn't impress them, I don't know what will."

Cooper knew he'd have to answer for the Coast Guard's pursuit and the loss of his boat at some point, but he hoped his accomplishments would outweigh those unfortunate events. Sam needed to hurry up and finish so they could get out of there. He turned to face his screen and began pounding on his keyboard, typing the script he would use to present his results.

Cooper lifted his head at the distant hum of an approaching helicopter. While still facing his screen, he said, "It sounds like Landry's flight is coming sooner than we expected." As the sound grew louder, he realized it was nearing their outpost instead. It had to be someone from the cartel. When it landed on their designated landing zone some distance from his encampment, he said, "We've got company," as he grabbed his parka and hurried toward the door. "Stay here and keep working."

While the helicopter blades were still spinning, a man wearing a business suit, jarringly out of place on the glacier, climbed out and walked awkwardly in smooth-soled shoes toward Cooper as he stood a few feet away. At first, he couldn't tell who it was in the deepening shadows. Then he recognized that his worst fear had been realized. It was Faisal.

"I warned you about security," Faisal shouted as he slipped and shuffled in his wingtips across the snow.

Trying to forestall what was sure to get ugly, Cooper said, "Come in and I'll show you around."

"I'm not here for a tour. Where's your assistant?"

Cooper pointed toward the shelters a hundred yards away. "I told her to wait inside."

"Good. My pilot can't hear, either, with his noise-cancelling headset on."

"You flew up here just to talk?"

"I said you'd pay a price for any leaks. You remember what has happened to reporters critical of the Saudi royal family?"

Cooper didn't respond and was pretty sure where the conversation was headed.

Faisal thrust a piece of paper at Cooper—the Coast Guard news release. "This," Faisal said shaking the paper, "is a massive leak. And I heard Homeland Security *and* the FBI are investigating."

"I've already seen it."

"How did you let this *happen*? The Coast Guard doesn't pursue random boats without a good reason."

Cooper had to make Faisal understand. "I had the same thought. Professor Landry from the University of Washington has been camping on the glacier near here." He pointed in the direction of Landry's encampment. "She's determined to find out what's causing the snowstorms. I thought I'd chased her off with the avalanche." He stretched out both arms and shrugged. "You remember? I sent the cartel photos of her demolished research station."

"So?"

"About ten days later, Landry returned, and I got the Park Service to revoke her permit to get resupplied. I even directed a major storm toward her flimsy tent."

Faisal stood frowning with his arms crossed across his chest. "Words. More words. I'm not convinced. Why do you suspect her?"

Cooper felt the sharp taste of stomach acid in his mouth as he tried to think of a way to avoid telling Faisal about Landry's visit and their conversation on the radio. He couldn't come up with anything other than the truth.

"Stop stalling, and don't lie to me. Tell me what you know." Faisal's jaw was clenched and his hand moved across a bulge in his suit coat that looked like a gun.

"Landry showed me photos she took of one of my cloud seeding generators." He shifted his weight from one foot to the other. "She discovered it somehow."

"What did you tell her?"

"I didn't deny it. I told her it was a method commonly used to squeeze precipitation from clouds. I then convinced her that the clouds formed naturally."

"That's bad enough, but how the hell did she find your boat?"

"I'm guessing she spotted the cloud patterns on satellite imagery and relayed coordinates for those points to the Coast Guard. Before they could board it, I had it take evasive maneuvers. When that didn't work, I blew it up and sank it."

Faisal got in Cooper's face and growled, "You stupid fool! Now the Coast Guard knows they were on to something illegal. And it won't take rocket science for Landry to put that fireworks display together with your cloud seeding and tie you to the boats." Faisal's huge hands curled into fists that Cooper pictured smashing his face. "Does she know we're adding sulfur to the jet fuel?"

Cooper shook his head.

Faisal grunted in disbelief. "Your so-called security is thin as a veil. She saw right through it." He ripped open his coat, revealing a shoulder holster with the biggest automatic pistol Cooper had ever seen. "Now you know what you must do?"

Cooper stared at the gun. He never expected his project would end in murder. "You want me to kill Landry before she figures out we're adding sulfur to jet fuel."

"*Yes.*" The word echoed over the glacier. "We don't care so much about your cloud seeding and your little boats. But the cartel has plans for deploying your jet fuel formula worldwide. We can't let Landry or anyone else interfere with that. Does Landry even suspect the jet fuel?"

"No." Cooper shifted his eyes away from the gun. "And she can't confirm anything—not even if she has suspicions."

"Good. Make her death convincing. There's probably lots of ways someone could die in a dangerous place like this." Faisal looked around at the snow-covered peaks.

Cooper focused on the snowy slope leading up to Snow Dome above his camp. "Landry's oblivious to the danger she's put herself in. All the new snow that's piled up above her tent on the side of Panic Peak could easily break loose with a little help."

"Make it happen—*tomorrow*! I'll be back to verify she's *dead*." Faisal's words echoed again and sent chills up Cooper's spine. "When I return, I'll want the jet fuel formula and your documentation of its effectiveness. Then we'll see if you deserve any of the money you expect." Faisal turned and walked unsteadily back toward his helicopter.

Cooper stood frozen as the copter's engine revved up and its blades began to spin. He felt exposed, standing alone on the barren snow. As the aircraft roared and lifted into the twilight, the word "catastrophe" flashed into his mind. What a catastrophe it had been to join forces with the cartel in the first place.

33

Caltech Research Site
Blue Glacier

Wednesday, July 13

Sam cracked open the door to the hut and stood behind it so she could hear the conversation between Cooper and the man who arrived by helicopter. Cooper had to be talking to someone from the cartel, but she could see only the silhouettes of two men who stood in the deep shadows. The tall, slender one looked like Cooper. The other man was short and stocky. Although they were a hundred yards away, the absence of sound from wind or the helicopter engine meant that the voices carried much farther than they might have in a different setting. The cold, dense air in contact with the snow may have increased the effect.

Cooper seemed to be trying to calm the visitor, who leaned in on Cooper. They were arguing about Dr. Landry. The word "security" slid across the snow to her. When she heard the words "kill," "dead," and "tomorrow," Sam's whole body started shaking. She couldn't pick out the details, but she got the gist. The big guy wanted Cooper to kill Kate. Would Cooper *do* that? She'd spent almost two years working for this man, and she'd lived and worked with him for months. She saw her boss and mentor as annoying, pompous, and sexist— but not a murderer. Now that he stood in the snow a football field distance away, it suddenly felt unsafe to be near him.

Sam's mind raced. Cooper didn't move as the helicopter levitated into the sky. What should she do? She couldn't just run away. Somehow, she had to pretend everything was normal. As soon as the helicopter flew off, he began walking fast toward the shelter.

She had to warn Landry. She turned from the doorway and flew past the instruments to grab the small radio transceiver from the back of Cooper's desk. Hurriedly and in hushed tones, she said, "Kate are you there? Do you hear me?"

A few tense seconds passed, and she heard static followed by, "I'm here, Sam. What's up?"

"You're in danger. Email me and I'll explain." She gave Kate her email address and dropped the transceiver on the desk just as Cooper walked through the canvas storm flap covering the door. When he saw her standing by his desk, he raised his eyebrows with a quizzical expression but didn't say anything. He was distracted, and his face telegraphed an unclear mixture of what might be fear, anger, or disgust.

She tried to sound nonchalant. "What was that about?"

Cooper's voice was tense. "That was Faisal, from the cartel. Checking on progress. Showed me a copy of the Coast Guard news release. Wondered if we knew about it."

"He flew all the way up here for that? What did you say?"

"I told him Landry threatened to reveal our weather modification, and he was furious. I told him she couldn't prove anything except the cloud seeding and that we've completed our studies. Starting to pack up. Need a few days to tie up loose ends."

"What do you mean by loose ends?" She suspected what he meant but tried to sound innocent.

Cooper glared at her with an expression she couldn't interpret. Impatience? Anger? Guilt? She couldn't hold his gaze and she couldn't move.

"Hey, Sam. Snap out of it!" He waved in her face, and she flinched and jumped backward. "We've got a ton of equipment to prepare for transport."

She was afraid for her life but tried hard not to show it. "Of course. It could take us days." She returned to her desk and pretended to work on the weather data charts.

Once Cooper sat down at his work station facing away from her, she addressed an email to Kate and began typing a quick note. When Cooper stood and walked toward her, she closed her email before he could read her screen.

"I thought you were compiling our data. What are you doing on email? Who were you writing?"

Without making eye contact, she said, "Just telling my mother I'll be home in a few days. I'll spend time with her in San Jose before going back to Caltech."

"Do that later! Get me the charts I need *now* so I can finish my presentation."

Sam was so rattled she could hardly breathe. She'd have to be more discreet and warn Kate somehow, but she couldn't control her voice and trembling body, let alone act normal in the presence of a man she now knew was capable of murder.

Cooper became increasingly agitated and began pacing like he had a few days earlier. Maybe that meant he wasn't a cold-blooded killer.

"What's the problem?" Sam asked tentatively. She was afraid of setting him off.

"I'm thinking of all the things I have to finish. Before . . . we . . . leave!"

He was clearly losing it. She had to send Kate an email.

Each time he walked away from her and toward the door, Sam typed a line in Kate's email. Each time he returned, she flipped to the data chart she was building. It was a ridiculous dance, but she couldn't risk getting caught.

Finally, she completed it and clicked the "Send" button. It simply read, "Cooper has orders to kill you from secret oil cartel, source of his funding. More to weather changes than you know. Afraid you'll discover everything. Don't know what he plans. Could be tomorrow."

Kate replied almost instantly. When Cooper wasn't looking, Sam opened the message and read, "You serious? When? How can I protect myself?"

When she was able to, Sam typed, "Will try to shadow him and warn you. Be prepared."

"Unbelievable! Thanks."

Sam had grown to admire Kate and her dogged determination for research, though it made Sam feel ashamed for compromising her values, including her concern about global warming. She stared at the data charts on her screen, but the content didn't even register. Why had she succumbed to Cooper's promise of money and prestige? She'd respected Cooper as a scientist and mentor. His brilliant mind and ambition had inspired her. But now he made her sick. She should have acted on her reservations about working for the cartel of oil executives. Now that she'd been spying for them, she was complicit in the whole mess. How could she have ever thought that would turn out okay? Cooper was a liar and a manipulator. And now a potential murderer. She had to help Kate and get as far away from him as she could—without getting herself killed too.

34

Kate Landry's Encampment
Blue Glacier

Wednesday, July 13

Alone in the shadow of Panic Peak in a small and battered tent, Kate felt small, exposed, and vulnerable as night approached. Sam's warning that Cooper planned to kill her kept repeating in her head. Could she even believe it? She hardly knew Samantha Schroeder. Besides, there was nowhere to hide for long, and the only weapons she could think of were her ice ax, a hammer, and her pocketknife. Knowing that Cooper was capable of blowing up boats to avoid detection, what might he do to her? A chill went up her spine. She rooted around her toolbox and pulled out the claw hammer and stared at it.

Could this possibly be a sick plan cooked up by Cooper and Sam together to scare Kate off the glacier? That also seemed plausible. But what if Sam *was* telling the truth and just didn't have a chance to explain? Her voice on the radio seemed sincere—and scared.

Kate's situation felt dire. She thought about calling Grant, but what could he do from so far away? It would only make him frantic. She loved him, but she might never see him again, and now she realized she'd been so preoccupied by her work that she hadn't even told him she loved him in some time.

Kate pushed thoughts of Grant out of her mind. She had to focus on staying alive so she and Grant would have another chance. And so she could expose Cooper. She blew out a huge breath.

As she considered her limited options, her mind raced and she became more agitated. Her pulse was racing and her breathing was rapid and shallow. When she touched her forehead, it was cold, clammy, and sweaty. She'd be in serious trouble if she didn't calm down. Taking charge of the situation was required, and the only real option that made sense was to leave. She could ski down to the tip of the ice and then hike out to the visitor center to get help.

Kate began piling clothes and food on her cot—things she would need for the twenty-five-mile trek. She considered the route she would take off Snow Dome to get past the Caltech encampment so Cooper wouldn't spot her. And she had to avoid crevasses and the icefall. It would be tricky and dangerous, but she couldn't wait for Cooper to make his move.

Then she remembered Sam. If she was telling the truth, she'd taken a risk by warning Kate about Cooper's intentions. She'd be equally vulnerable. She had to include Sam in her plans for escape. As far as she knew, Sam didn't have ski equipment or any experience skiing on a glacier. Remembering all the difficulties she and Grant had hiking down the steep and rough trail the year before, that option was not appealing either.

Escaping by helicopter made more sense. Now that she'd decided to leave anyway, she had really nothing to lose by asking the rangers to fly her and Sam out. She'd call park headquarters. If she could talk to Ben and tell him someone was planning on killing her, he'd be there in a flash. She picked up her cell phone but saw that the network was down again. "Damn," she said out loud. "Of all times . . ." She had to call somehow and thought of the handheld Park Service radio. Although it was late, a ranger might be on duty. She hadn't tested her radio since she arrived. Would the battery still be charged? She turned it on and hoped for the best. "National Park headquarters. This is Dr. Kate Landry on Blue Glacier. I need emergency assistance." She waited seated stiffly at her desk, holding the radio to her lips. No response. "Anyone in Olympic National Park, please respond."

After an anxious minute, she heard, "Dr. Landry, this is Ranger Michael Long at the Hoh Rain Forest Visitor Center. We met last summer. How can I help?"

Kate jumped to her feet. "Oh, Michael, so good to hear you. I know it's late, but could you get Ben Johnson to come on? I'm dealing with an emergency up here and need his help."

"Sure. Stand by."

Kate paced in a tight circle around the tent. When Ben's voice boomed through her radio and she identified herself, he immediately asked what was wrong.

She was about to cry from relief at just hearing Ben's voice. "I need your help. I'll keep it short." Her voice trembled. "Do you know I'm back on Blue Glacier?"

"We need to change channels so the entire Park Service doesn't hear us. Switch to channel three on your unit. I'll meet you there."

After they switched channels, Ben said, "I heard that you're no longer working for U-Dub. Is that true?"

"It is. But Ben, I'm stuck." Her words came tumbling out, clipped and fast. "No Park Service waiver. Pilot refuses to take me off mountain."

"Take it easy," Ben said. "Breathe."

She began talking more slowly. "Dr. Mark Cooper has been doing research here since January."

"I'm aware. He's got the same waiver you had."

"He's been modifying the weather up here since September. That's why we had the extreme weather that caused the family to drown."

"That I didn't know. Go on."

"I'll spare the details." Kate stood at her desk. "I just learned Cooper's planning to kill me."

"*Kill* you? Why?"

"Because I discovered his illegal activities. Sam, his assistant, warned me. She said it will be tonight or tomorrow."

"Has *he* threatened you?"

"No, but he sank a boat when the Coast Guard approached to investigate. He's dangerous."

"I'm sending an armed ranger to pick you up and bring in Cooper for questioning."

"How soon can they get here?"

"First thing in the morning. It's too dangerous to fly in the mountains at night."

"Thanks. I just hope he doesn't try anything tonight."

"Me too. That's the best I can do."

"And Ben, one more thing. Would you call Grant for me if anything bad happens?" She gave him Grant's cell number and ended the call. Now, without her connection to Ben's reassuring voice, Kate sat on the edge of her cot knowing she'd have to face the dark, cold night completely on her own.

35

Panic Peak
Olympic National Park

Thursday, July 14

The snow glowed a cool white as the light of a full moon reflected off the surface of Snow Dome. Cooper straightened up from where he worked on the side of Panic Peak—burying dynamite in the ice. He could see Landry's tent far below. In another hour, at sunrise, his explosives would trigger a massive avalanche of snow, ice, and rock that would roar down the side of the mountain, obliterating Landry's camp and crushing her inside.

Weeks ago, when creating the small explosion for his first avalanche, his intent had been to scare Landry and force her to leave. This time was different. She would leave, all right, but in a body bag. If and when her body could be recovered. He regretted the deaths of the family of four, whose car had washed into the overflowing Hoh River soon after his geoengineering had increased precipitation on Mount Olympus. He'd read about the whole mess on the internet, but he wasn't actually responsible for that family's deaths. Not directly anyway. They had driven into the flood.

His hands shook, and he felt a sense of doom as he attached the last wires between the radio receiver and the detonator on the bundle of high explosives. How had his intense desire to save the planet from global warming come to this? He swore then and there that this would be the last illegal act he would commit for the cartel. He knew the explosive residue might be traced, but he hoped no one would suspect his involvement.

The beam of a flashlight near Kate's tent distracted him, and he ducked instinctively. It was Landry walking to the privy where she'd erected a rough shelter of broken boards from the shed. He remained crouched and hidden until she returned to her tent.

Faisal was right that once Landry had figured out the plot, she would tell the FBI, and word would reach the public. She'd already gotten the Coast Guard involved. But it was a waste of a smart scientist. Still, Landry had put herself in harm's way by returning to the glacier. She didn't have the sense to quit after she nearly died in his first avalanche. Landry was so goddamned stubborn. He'd tried to warn her. He'd told her to stop, but she refused to listen.

Cooper flipped the switch to activate the remote detonator in his hand, and the light on top turned green. The receiver was armed and ready to set off the massive explosion. An accidental twitch of his thumb and the spot where he stood would be obliterated. Sweat beaded on his forehead. Maybe that would be for the best. This whole mess would just be over—fast. He took several shaky breaths and watched them billow in the icy night air. It would be so easy to press the button. He abruptly toggled off the remote and slid it into his pocket.

Ever since Faisal's visit and threat, Cooper realized how short-sighted he'd been. The cartel didn't give a rat's ass about causing this one glacier to grow. They wanted his formula for adding sulfur to jet fuel so they could deploy it throughout their worldwide distribution channels. Their goal was to cool the entire planet so they could continue selling petroleum. So he, Mark Claude

Cooper, was enabling the buildup of greenhouse gases, not saving the planet. Sooner or later, this would all lead to the mass extinction of plants and animals and the deaths of hundreds of thousands, if not millions, of people. But wasn't it too late to stop what he'd already set in motion?

He spotted another movement near Landry's tent and snapped up the binoculars hanging by a strap around his neck. But this time, it was someone else. Someone was walking down the side of Snow Dome directly toward the tent. He focused on the moving figure, and he recognized Sam's long stride. He held his breath. Why would Sam be visiting Landry? But there was something else. She kept looking up in his direction. She must have guessed he was planning an avalanche and followed him here. She was going to warn Landry. How stupid of her. A person couldn't help but stand out against the white snow, even in this moonlight. He watched her arrive at the tent, hesitate, and go inside.

Cooper could barely breathe as his chest tightened with the betrayal. The ungrateful bitch! He'd supported her career and put up with her snippy attitude. Fueled by rage, Cooper began charging down the side of Panic Peak, taking huge strides in his snowshoes.

36

Kate Landry's Encampment
Blue Glacier

Thursday, July 14

Kate sat at her table uploading all her data and notes to cloud storage, praying that the internet signal would hold until she finished. She planned to email instructions to Grant for how to access it so it wouldn't be lost if she was killed. She hadn't slept and wasn't even sleepy. All she could focus on was getting ready to leave when the rangers arrived. And she kept her ice ax with her at all times, even when she went out to use the privy.

She was just checking her watch—just past four—when she heard a loud whisper calling her name outside the tent. Gripping the ice ax, she stood up and opened the tent flap a crack. It was Sam, wide-eyed and panicked. She put her fingers to her lips and motioned for Sam to come in.

Once inside, Sam blurted out, "Cooper's above us on Panic Peak. I've been following him for about an hour."

"What's he doing?"

"Digging! Burying something in the snow. I'm afraid he's about to trigger an avalanche to kill you."

Kate's heart pounded. "Start an avalanche? How?"

"Like that avalanche that buried your research station. I think Cooper caused it."

"But I felt the vibration from the generator's flywheel."

"I know. But Cooper was acting strange then. And now he's planting something on Panic Peak in the middle of the night."

There was no time to spare. Kate set down the ice ax, shut her laptop, stuffed it into her pack, and wrestled it onto her back. "Your email mentioned a cartel. Did *they* tell Cooper to kill me?"

Sam nodded. "They've paid him to test a sulfur dioxide shield to cool the climate so they can sell more petroleum. They have trillions of dollars at stake."

"A sulfur dioxide shield? Is Cooper using commercial jets to deploy it?"

"Yes. The cartel's adding sulfur to fuel going to Sea-Tac."

"I knew it!" Kate pounded her fist into her palm. "But now you're in danger too."

"Yeah." Sam turned. "I'd better get back before Cooper discovers I'm here. You should get out too."

"And why should she get out of here?" A deep voice boomed as Cooper threw open the tent flap. Kate and Sam both jumped. Then they froze. Cooper glared at Sam, and Kate began backing away in the direction of her ice ax. She'd take him on in hand-to-hand combat if necessary.

"What are you doing here?" Cooper demanded of Sam.

"What were *you* doing on Panic Peak in the middle of the night?" Kate countered.

Sam faced Cooper with her chin out in defiance. "I warned Kate."

"You're a total fraud, Cooper," Kate said. "You created all the weather changes you claimed to be studying."

"You warned Landry about what?"

"You don't owe him an explanation, Sam," Kate said as she touched the blade of the ice ax with her right hand.

Cooper lurched toward Sam with outstretched arms, as if he meant to strangle her. "Ungrateful traitor!"

At that moment, Kate hoisted her ice ax in both hands and aimed at Cooper's skull.

Cooper threw up his hands and yelled, "Stop, Landry!" Then he started backing toward the entrance.

Kate lunged forward, and Cooper lost his balance, falling back against the tent pole that Kate had repaired during the storm. The ski-pole splint snapped and the nylon tent collapsed on him. As he fought the fabric to get free, two more tent poles fell inward. Suddenly all three scientists were thrashing under the loose fabric, trying to get loose. Kate had lost the tactical advantage she'd had seconds before.

"You're a threat to us all, Landry," Cooper yelled while attempting to stand.

"Shut the fuck up," Kate shot back.

"Okay, stop!" Sam ordered. "On three everyone stand up together. One—two—three!"

They managed to lift the tent up enough to stand.

"Use the good posts to prop it up," shouted Kate. She lifted a pole and repositioned it in the corner while keeping an eye on Cooper. Sam did the same with a second pole.

Cooper hoisted his end of the tent. "What have you got to hold this piece of shit up?"

"Use this," Kate said as she remembered the aluminum pole she used to measure snow depth and slid out a length of it from the floor of the tent behind the bed. Cooper wedged it up at an angle. It was enough to hold up the fabric temporarily.

Kate glared at Cooper with her ice ax across her chest, ready to raise it again. "If you threaten us again, I'll put this through your skull. Now talk. And no bullshit."

"Listen to me, Landry," Cooper said while stretching both hands out, palms up. "You and I aren't so different. I saw how excited you got when you learned your glacier was expanding. I made that happen. And I've perfected methods to remove greenhouse gases from the atmosphere. I can solve global warming. Did Sam tell you?"

"No. Just tell us what you've done."

He narrowed his eyes at Kate. "You can hate me for accepting money from the only people who offered it. Their petroleum dollars will dry up sooner or later, so I figured, why not use them to solve the problem instead of sitting on my hands?"

Kate stared, waiting for Cooper to explain all he had done. Sam rolled her eyes like she'd heard it all before.

He snorted. "If we don't do something now, human life will vanish in a couple hundred years." He looked at Kate. "I tried to make you leave, but demolishing your research station didn't work. Did Sam tell you I caused the avalanche?"

"Yes."

Cooper's shoulders slumped. "Since you came back, this is how bad it's gotten." He pulled the remote detonator from his pocket.

She stared at it. "That was meant for me?" Kate asked.

Cooper didn't respond.

Sam yelled, "Oh, my God. He's planning to kill us all!"

Cooper looked down at the remote and shook his head. "No, Sam. I'm not." Then he looked at Kate, his forehead wrinkled.

"If you're trying to threaten me for my silence, it won't work. I'm not like you. I have moral standards."

Cooper smirked. "All you have to do is go off and quietly teach geology at some small college. No one will be the wiser. At least *you* will have a future."

"Go to hell! You're the one who's sold his soul to the greedy oil barons."

"And I'm through working for you!" Sam yelled, pounding on Kate's table.

"I've already arranged for Sam and me to be picked up this morning," Kate said levelly. "You can just answer to your oil-loving buddies by yourself."

Cooper looked from Sam to Kate and then said, "Faisal told me yesterday that the cartel plans to supply jet fuel to the major airlines worldwide. They think they can deliver my formula without being detected. Their operations are scattered through so many subsidiaries, it would be impossible to track back to the source."

Kate shook her head in disbelief. "I can think of fifty reasons why that would be a disaster, starting with the total disruption of the cloud and rainfall patterns around the world."

Sam nodded. "Ocean acidification and groundwater contamination too."

Kate held the ice ax at the ready across her chest, but all that was left to do was wait. And worry. Kate glanced at her watch. In just nine minutes, everything had changed. But instead of getting ready to be rescued off Blue Glacier by rangers in a helicopter, she had Sam to protect. And they would leave Cooper to deal with some god-awful, greedy cartel. It was a good thing she was running on adrenaline because it was the only thing holding off the exhaustion.

The rising sun was sending a blush of light into the sky. She hoped this would be the last day she ever had to talk to Cooper. For the moment, though, she forced herself to keep talking in hopes of learning what he had planned. She still considered him a threat.

"How much time do we have before your guy returns?"

"He's not my guy. We've got some time. He's waiting to receive my coded message that my avalanche obliterated your site with you inside." He held up the remote detonator.

"Put that thing away before it goes off," Kate said, glancing again at her watch. "So we've got time to come up with a plan. How can we stop the cartel from distributing sulfur-laced fuel?"

Cooper shook his head. "We can't. The cartel controls the production and distribution, but we could stop the deployment at the airports."

"How?" Sam asked.

Cooper hesitated. "My formula has two unique properties. One is to protect nickel-based jet engine alloys from the corrosive oxides produced when sulfur burns. The other is to mask the sulfur during the screening that every airport uses to ensure their fuel has low sulfur content. If we can eliminate the effectiveness of the masking, then every commercial airport already has the equipment needed to detect the contraband fuel and block it. It's a matter of changing the spectrum of the sensing electronics to reveal the hidden sulfur in my formula. I have recorded the modifications that would be required on my computer."

Kate nodded. "That would mean retrofitting equipment at every airport, but it would prevent the disastrous deployment of sulfur. Then every delivery could be detected and stopped before it could do any damage."

"But what about the man from the cartel—Faisal?" Sam asked. "What do we do once that goon finds out you haven't killed Kate?"

"That's a hard one. He's unpredictable and dangerous. He threatened my life when he told me to murder Landry."

"What can we use to defend ourselves?" Sam asked.

"All I've got is my ice ax, a hammer, and my pocket knife," Kate said. "Do you have anything at your camp we could use as a weapon?"

Cooper shrugged. "Just more tools."

Kate tipped her head, listening. "Wait! I think I hear the Park Service helicopter." The rhythmic beat of an approaching aircraft grew louder.

"That would be our ride out of here." Kate grinned at Sam.

"I need them to take me too," Cooper said. "I don't want to deal with Faisal again."

"You'd have to ask them. But they're going to arrest you first." Kate started stuffing the clothes piled on the cot into her canvas duffel.

All three turned their heads as the sound grew louder. Then suddenly, it went silent.

"Shit! I'll bet it's Faisal," Cooper said. "Probably landed at our camp."

Sam's eyes were wide with panic. "Maybe he'll think we're out in the field and leave," she said doubtfully.

"I doubt it," Cooper said. "You don't know how determined he is. He'll fly up here to see if the avalanche covered Kate's tent. We can't hide. He can come after us with the helicopter." Cooper kept swallowing nervously.

"Arm yourselves." Kate handed Sam the hammer then picked up her ice ax. She nodded at Cooper. "I suggest you keep that detonator handy. Your dynamite might be our last resort."

Cooper's face turned pale. After about five minutes, the helicopter approached, and the downdraft from the rotor whipped Kate's tent. She grabbed onto one of the support poles to keep the tent from collapsing again. The helicopter landed some distance away.

Cooper peeked out the tent flap. "Faisal's coming, but the pilot's still inside." Cooper's voice rose in pitch. "We'll overpower him. It's three against one." He sounded desperate.

Kate couldn't see a way out. "Nice goons you work for. You got us into this, now you get us out."

A heavyset man wearing black ski pants and an orange parka tore back the tent flap and charged in. "Well, look who's here: the whole crew." He leaned into Cooper but had to look up to his face. "Is this how you eliminate the threat, Cooper? You've made my job a lot easier."

Faisal pulled his automatic pistol from under his parka and pointed it at Kate. "Is this the one who's giving us all the trouble?"

"Oh, God," Sam cried, clapping her hand over her mouth.

Faisal pointed the gun at Cooper. "Give me the formula," Faisal growled.

"Cooper, don't do it," Kate yelled. "You can't trust him."

"Send it to my encrypted account," Faisal said with a crooked grin and handed him a card with account information. "Then I'll be gone."

Cooper moved toward Kate's laptop, which was still logged on to the internet. "I have no choice," he said in a weak voice.

"Don't," she shouted. "He'll kill us anyway."

Cooper paid no attention and typed while Kate glared at Faisal and his big-ass gun, wondering what she could do next.

"It's done," Cooper said as he sent it.

Faisal pulled up a satellite phone that was clipped to his waist and spoke to someone in Arabic. "Okay, we've received it. Now we're all going for a little hike up the side of this mountain behind us."

Kate shook her head. Just as she'd predicted.

"I sent you the formula," Cooper said as he walked up to Faisal and stood in his face. "You said you'd be gone."

Faisal sneered and pushed him back with the barrel of his pistol. "I'll be gone—after the three of you have an unfortunate climbing accident." He pointed the gun at Kate. "What's behind your back?"

She lifted her ice ax and handed it to him.

"Let me see what's in your pockets, Cooper." Faisal frisked him and took out the remote for the explosives. "We might use this after all. You can show me where you planted the explosives." He turned to Sam. "What are you holding behind *your* back?"

Sam slowly handed him the hammer with a look of disgust.

"I can see you were planning for a fight. We're going for a little climb instead."

Kate's mind raced. They were almost out of options. The only thing she could think of to save their lives was to look for an opportunity to overpower Faisal. He was clueless about the topography and snowshoeing, but his advantage was the gun. But with Faisal holding them at gunpoint, she had no idea how to share her plan with Cooper and Sam.

They all stood outside putting on their snowshoes while Faisal walked the few feet to the helicopter and spoke with the pilot.

Seizing the opportunity, Kate whispered to Cooper and Sam, "Let's overpower him when we can. I'll give the cue."

Cooper and Sam nodded, their looks a mixture of resignation and fear. It was a relief to see Faisal return alone. It would have been nearly impossible to overcome him and the pilot together.

Soon Kate and the others were silently climbing up the steep snow-covered incline of Panic Peak. The three scientists were tied at intervals along the climbing rope, which apparently was Faisal's idea for making it look like an accident when their bodies were discovered. The rope dragged over the snow. Sam was in the lead, followed by Kate. Faisal pointed his gun at Cooper, who was last on the rope. The early morning sun to the east created a blinding reflection off the snow, and Kate started sweating from the combined sunlight, exertion, and fear.

The mountain became so steep that even with snowshoes, their feet slid backwards with each step. As they neared the top, the path grew narrower, so when Kate looked to the right, she peered down into the deep ravine. Turning to the left, she could make out parts of White Glacier two thousand feet below. She could see why Faisal had chosen Panic Peak for their murder. There were drop-offs of hundreds of feet in many spots. She tried not to think about that and looked for opportunities to overpower him.

Kate spotted places where deep snowdrifts had formed, blown by the westerly winds. Some extended over the edge of the ravine to form overhanging cornices, which were more easily visible from below as she climbed and knew what to look for. From above, cornices looked like ordinary snowdrifts, so someone might walk out onto one without realizing that it could easily break off, causing a fall of a hundred feet or more.

When they'd started climbing, the cornices were far away, but as they approached the summit, their path took them closer to the overhangs. This could be it—their last hope for escape. Kate hoped Faisal wouldn't realize the danger lurking nearby.

Up ahead, she saw a particularly large cornice that had cracks beginning to form where it had begun to break off. She stopped next to it and pretended to adjust the binding on her snowshoes. As Cooper and Faisal caught up to her, she sprang up shouting, "*Now!*" and threw her body sideways into Faisal. He lost his balance and fell closer to the edge. The gun fired wildly into the air. Cooper dove on top of Faisal, wrestling with him for the gun while Sam stood paralyzed.

In spite of their combined weight, the cornice didn't break off as Kate had hoped, and Faisal had landed too far from the edge of the cliff to push him over. She dove on top of his legs, trying to hold him long enough for Cooper to wrestle the gun away. Meanwhile, Sam snapped out of her trance and grabbed one of Faisal's arms.

The four struggled in the snow, a confusion of arms, legs, and shouts. Then the gun fired again. The noise pierced Kate's ears, and she instinctively tried to cover them with her hands. Then she noticed that Cooper had stopped moving. He lay on top of Faisal, blood oozing from a wound in his back.

Sam screamed, "No!" and began pounding Faisal on the head with her snowshoe.

Kate was overcome by anger, and she lit into Faisal with complete, insane abandon. She kicked him with her snowshoes and pounded him with her fists. But more than trying to save her life, she fought to save the planet. At all costs, she had to stop the cartel from deploying Cooper's formula.

With the thrashing of the bodies, Kate felt the cornice shift. The crack on its side grew wider. Just a little more and Faisal would go over the edge. While Faisal struggled to push Cooper's body off him and free his gun, Kate yelled to Sam, "Get back!" Then she leapt up and landed on the cornice in her snowshoes. The snow under Faisal tipped farther and he slid out from under Cooper's body, which remained anchored on the snow next to Sam. As Faisal struggled to sit and aim his gun, the cornice broke free and plummeted with a sharp crack. Kate and Faisal both dropped toward the ravine.

In desperation, Kate twisted her torso to face the cliff, reached out, and grabbed a protruding rock. There she dangled by one arm as she heard Faisal's scream from below, ending abruptly in a muffled whump as his body hit the snow, triggering an avalanche. Glancing down, she saw the avalanche carry Faisal's orange and black form, with arms and legs moving wildly, before covering it in a deep overlay of packed, concrete-hard snow.

Kate pulled with all her strength to rise up high enough to grab something with her free hand, but she couldn't do it. Desperately trying to keep from losing her grip, she looked down and saw a narrow ledge of rock below her, now exposed after the cornice had fallen away. If only she could land there without falling backward. She began swinging her legs and let go when she thought her body was aimed right. After dropping about ten feet and painfully hitting the ledge with both feet, she nearly lost her balance. Abruptly, she dropped to her knees, bringing her center of gravity down closer to the ledge.

She had saved herself from sharing Faisal's fate, but now she was stranded about fifteen feet below the rim on Panic Peak. "Sam, I'm not hurt. Are you okay?" she shouted.

"I'm fine, but I think Cooper is dead." Kate could hear her crying. "He's bleeding a lot, and I don't think he's breathing. I hated his guts, but I didn't want him to die."

"I know, Sam, but I need your help. You and I are still attached to each other by the climbing rope. Do you know how to perform a belay?"

"No. I've just heard the term."

"Look for a large boulder or outcrop a few feet back from the edge. Sit down behind it with your feet braced against the rock. Then run the climbing rope around your back and up over your shoulder to hold it across your chest. You can take up the slack as I climb and hold my weight in case I fall. Does that make sense?"

"I think so," Sam replied.

Kate removed her snowshoes and stuck them in her backpack. While Sam got ready, she studied the rock face in front of her. There were a few spots where she could plant her feet, but nothing looked substantial enough to support her full weight. She spotted a crack in the rock running vertically from the ledge she was on to near the top. That had potential and would have to do.

"I've found a boulder. I'm in position behind it," Sam shouted.

"Good. I'm climbing."

Kate wedged the toe of her left boot into the opening as far as she could and put both hands into the crack at chest height, pulling with all her strength in opposite directions to give her leverage. She lifted her right boot in the crack a foot higher and slid both hands up, maintaining as much pressure as she could.

She called up to Sam, "Keep the rope taut. I can barely hold my weight." Just then, Kate's boot slipped, and her handholds alone couldn't keep her up. She slid down the rock face, held only by the rope clipped to her climbing harness.

She yelled up, "Sam, can you hold me?"

"I think so," Sam called through gritted teeth. "Hurry!"

"Lower me back down to the ledge."

Kate studied the rock face in front of her again, desperately looking for another route. She noticed a rock slab with a slight lip at the top that began about five feet to her left and angled up to near the top. That slab started so far from the ledge she'd have to swing over to it on the rope.

"Sam, you've got to hold my weight while I swing to a new position."

"I'll try."

"You've *got* to. If I slip, there's nothing to grab onto. Okay, here I go."

Kate moved to the far end of the ledge and made a running leap up and to her left. She grabbed the lip at the top of the slab just barely with the fingertips of both hands. Applying what friction she could from the soles of her boots against the rock, she began moving diagonally to the right up the rock slab. As she neared the top, she found good enough handholds to climb more easily. Sam kept taking up the slack in the rope, giving Kate what support she could.

Kate hoisted herself up over the top of the rock slab and lay back, alive but trying to comprehend what had just happened.

37

Panic Peak
Olympic National Park

Thursday, July 14

Kate peered cautiously over the edge into the ravine. "No sign of Faisal," she said between gasps for breath.

Sam knelt in the snow next to Cooper's lifeless form, crying softly as a sickening pool of blood darkened the snow.

"Faisal's body triggered a slide," Kate said. "All I see is the rough snow from an avalanche." She walked back to Sam and knelt next to her. Neither spoke. Kate put her arm around the distraught woman and said, "He made some . . . some bad choices. But you did the right thing by warning me. That saved both of us." She took a deep breath and puffed it out. The adrenaline was still pumping through her body and she needed to keep moving. "We've got to go. The park rangers are coming soon, and they'll take care of Cooper's body."

Sam got up. "He was so brilliant. And so, so stupid."

Kate strapped on her snowshoes and led Sam back down the steep slope of Panic Peak, taking large strides. Her whole body was tense, and she felt weak after the trauma of her close call. Faisal's helicopter was still parked far below where it had landed near Kate's tent. She worried that the pilot waiting inside might also be armed, but as the Park Service helicopter approached and circled overhead, Faisal's pilot took off and zoomed away. Eager for the help, Kate was relieved to see two rangers climbing out, each carrying a rifle.

Kate and Sam waved their arms and shouted, picking up their pace down the slope, and the rangers charged up the hill toward them.

As they approached, one of the rangers asked, "Which of you is Dr. Landry? Ranger Ben Johnson said your lives were in danger."

"That's me. We're so glad you're here, although we've taken care of the immediate threat. A man named Faisal was going to kill us near the summit of Panic Peak." Kate pointed with her thumb behind her. "He shot and killed Dr. Mark Cooper, but before he could shoot the two of us, I was able to push him off a cliff, and he fell into a ravine. The resulting avalanche buried his body. You'll need to retrieve both bodies."

"We'll handle it, ma'am. Do either of you need medical attention?"

"No," Kate said. "We're shaken but otherwise okay."

"Ranger Johnson wanted us to have you call him. But first, we need to get a statement from both of you about what happened."

Once near her tent, Kate described the events of that morning to the ranger who had done most of the talking, the helicopter pilot. She warned him about the explosive device and the remote detonator in Cooper's pocket that needed to be deactivated. He told Kate that they were instructed by Ben to fly them both to Port Angeles, where they would take them to meet him at the Olympic National Park Visitor Center.

The other ranger had taken Sam over to their helicopter to get her statement, and Kate turned for a moment to see them.

The ranger seemed very focused on taking notes while Sam spoke animatedly.

After she finished talking with the ranger, Kate stuffed her backpack with clothes and put her laptop in its case. When Sam joined her in the tent, Kate asked, "Do you need to go to your camp to shut down and secure things?"

"Yes. I've got to retrieve my computer with all my data. I should get Cooper's too. Can't risk having the cartel come back and steal everything."

"Let's ask the rangers to land there on our way back to Port Angeles. I can help you shut things down."

The women rode the short distance in the helicopter to the Caltech encampment, where Sam powered off the equipment, packed the two computers, and locked the shelters.

Looking down on the tip of the lower glacier as they left for Port Angeles, Kate saw the thick layer of snow still blanketing the ice. She knew the days would get warmer without Cooper's interventions and the snow would melt, exposing blue ice again. She turned in her seat and her eyes lingered on the snow covering the side of Mount Olympus where she'd spent years documenting the glacier's fate and pouring her heart and soul into teaching her students. She felt her eyes brim with tears when she realized this could be the last time she'd see her glacier.

38

Bill Fairchild Terminal
Port Angeles Airport

Thursday, July 14

Grant paced the tarmac outside the small terminal at the Port Angeles airport. The exhaust fumes from a departing jet were nauseating, but he didn't want to go back inside. Every time he heard the sounds of an incoming aircraft, he searched the sky, hoping it was the helicopter that would deliver Kate safely to him. He had to see she was all right with his own eyes. Over the last few weeks, they'd been struggling with the distance between them. But in the last twelve hours, the fear that she could die had changed everything.

Four years ago, death had carved a bottomless hole of grief and regret inside him when his fiancée had drowned in a boating accident. He might have saved her if he'd decided to go sailing with her instead of avoiding the scary waves that day. He never thought he would find love again until he met Kate. This time, he would be there for her, whatever it took. He'd caught a red-eye from Denver to Seattle and miraculously made it in time to meet Kate. He could hardly wait to see her again after all the weeks of distance between them.

When the green Park Service helicopter finally landed, Grant saw Kate's sunburned face behind the bubble canopy. She transformed from wide-eyed surprise to the biggest grin he'd ever seen. After jumping down from her seat, she waved and then ran toward him. Grant flew toward her, his arms outstretched, and they embraced hard. Kate's shoulders relaxed into him, her face buried into his chest. He held her for a few moments, rocking her. As they pulled apart a few inches, he wiped at the tears streaming down her cheeks. "You're here," he said.

"*You're* here." She dabbed her eyes with her sleeve. "I wasn't . . ."

"I'm so sorry." His voice cracked. "I'm so glad . . ."

"I thought we'd never . . ." Her face wrinkled as a new wave of tears began.

"I wasn't being supportive. I'm so sorry." He pulled her back into his chest and kissed the top of her head.

"I'm sorry too," she whispered.

"I don't want to lose you." He pulled her closer.

"I don't want to lose you either." Kate pulled back a little and searched his face. "How did you know I'd be here?"

"Ben. He told me the whole story. I got the first flight to Seattle this morning, rented a car, and here I am."

"That's like you—make a decision and move." Kate chuckled through her tears.

"Anywhere you need me." He kissed her again. Being with Kate once more and seeing her safe but vulnerable made him want to hold her and never let her go.

"Let me introduce you to the others." Kate led Grant over to the helicopter where the two rangers were helping Sam unload.

"This is my partner, Grant Poole, who just flew in from Denver," she said, holding his hand. "We met on Blue Glacier last summer when he was assessing my students' teamwork."

Grant shook hands with the rangers. Sam looked even younger than Kate had described.

"Kate told me about you on the flight from the glacier," Sam said, extending her hand.

Grant smiled. "Your brave actions saved Kate. Thank you."

Grant held the door open leading to the terminal while Kate and Sam carried their bags and laptops inside. A lone ticket agent was seated at a counter along one wall, and a woman, dressed in a business suit, appeared to be waiting inside for them. She walked up to Kate. "Are you Dr. Landry? I'm Agent Sasani from the Seattle Field Office of the FBI." She showed Kate her badge.

"Yes, I'm Kate Landry."

"I'm sorry to surprise you with so little warning, but I need to question you and Samantha Schroeder." She turned to face Sam. "Are you Ms. Schroeder?"

"Yes."

"I need the two of you to come with me to the Seattle office to be interviewed about the deaths on Mt. Olympus and Dr. Cooper's research activities. It won't take long."

Kate raised her eyebrows. "We weren't expecting you. How did you know we'd arrive this morning?"

"The FBI is in close contact with the Park Service." She looked over at the rangers. "We were told to expect you. Again, I'm sorry we couldn't give you more notice."

Kate set down her bags. "Agent Sasani, do we have to do this right *now*? Sam and I were nearly killed, and we need something to eat and time to recover."

The agent smiled broadly. "I know a café near here where we can get you something to eat. They make the best blueberry pancakes. You and Sam can take a nap in the back seat on the way to Seattle if you want."

One of the rangers stepped forward and said to the agent, "I'm sorry, ma'am, but we have orders to take Dr. Landry and Ms. Schroeder to Olympic National Park headquarters for a meeting with Chief Ranger Ben Johnson. He's expecting them."

Sasani smiled and said, "Please tell Ranger Johnson that we're sorry, but we must interview them first. We'd be happy to take them to the park headquarters to meet with him as soon as we're finished."

Grant knew the FBI had been informed by the Coast Guard about Cooper's boat that sank, but this was a bit much. He wedged himself between Kate and the agent. "Let's clear this with Ranger Johnson before you take Dr. Landry and Ms. Schroeder."

She looked up at Grant and stopped smiling. "I'm sorry. Who are you?"

Kate stood next to Grant. "Agent Sasani, this is a colleague of mine, Dr. Grant Poole."

"I'm sorry, but this doesn't involve you, Dr. Poole." She looked past Grant and addressed Kate and Sam. "Dr. Landry, Ms. Schroeder, would you like to use the ladies' room before we take the hour-long drive to Seattle?" She gestured toward the restrooms, and both Kate and Sam nodded. "And don't worry, we'll straighten this out with Ranger Johnson."

Kate and Sam followed her. As Kate reached the restroom door, she turned and shrugged, looking Grant's way. "I'll see you in a minute."

Grant waited with the two rangers while one called Ben at the Olympic National Park Visitor Center. The ranger calling looked over at Grant and said he was on hold while Ben called the Seattle office of the FBI to see what was going on.

Grant was irritated. He'd barely had time to say hello, and now she had to be in some kind of meeting for who knew how long. He tapped his foot impatiently, wondering why the women were taking so long in the restroom as he waited to hear what Ben had to say.

"*What*?" The ranger exclaimed into the phone. "Yes, sir. We will." He turned to the other ranger and blurted out, "She's an imposter—that supposed Agent Sasani woman."

Grant and the rangers barged into the restroom and searched the stalls. They were all empty, but the employee service entrance door to the outside was standing wide open.

Grant rushed out and watched as a black SUV roared out of the parking area, tires squealing. He got a glimpse of Kate and Sam in the back seat and two large men in the front next to the phony agent as she steered the car onto the street and sped away.

"We can't let them get away," Grant yelled as he started to move toward the parking lot. "Let's use my car."

A ranger grabbed his arm and gestured down the runway. "The helicopter." All three men sprinted across the tarmac toward the green helicopter parked outside.

39

Park Service Helicopter
Port Angeles Airport

Thursday, July 14

The two rangers took their positions in the front seat of the helicopter and Grant crawled into the rear. Within three minutes, they were airborne after the pilot announced their departure on the radio. After three more minutes, they flew above the only road out of Port Angeles toward the east.

Grant was so angry that someone would kidnap Kate right under his nose that he could barely breathe. He couldn't let those bastards get away, and he was sure it was the cartel. If, as Ben had told him, Cooper was killed by someone from an oil cartel and that man died trying to kill Kate and Sam, then this woman impersonating Agent Sasani must have also been sent by the cartel. And she was probably planning to finish the botched murder. Grant couldn't sit still knowing Kate's life was in imminent danger. Again.

He was connected through his intercom headset to the other two men. "They'll probably kill Kate and Sam the first chance they get. We've got to find them. How did you know which way they'd go?"

The pilot turned back toward Grant. "There are only two roads to the mainland from here. The western route's much longer, so I guessed they would drive east. Call out if you see the black SUV."

"I see lots of black cars and two black SUV's up ahead," the second ranger said.

"Keep looking."

The pilot maneuvered the helicopter directly over and slightly behind the SUVs. "I don't want to tip them off by getting too close. Let's see what they do from here."

Grant craned his neck to look down and pointed. "That one's passing all the other traffic."

"Jeez. They just ran a red light. Almost got hit broadside," the ranger said. "That's got to be them."

"I'll contact Seattle Flight Service and have them notify the police in Port Townsend," the pilot said. "All we can do is track them. The police will do the rest."

The pilot told Seattle Flight Service about the kidnaping and the urgency for police help. He also reported the location and approximate speed of the vehicle. After a couple of minutes, Flight Service told him they had notified the Port Townsend Police and the Washington State Highway Patrol in Bremerton.

After tracking the vehicle a few minutes more, Grant asked, "What town are they in now?"

"Sequim," the pilot said. "From here there are two ways off the peninsula. They could stay on the highway headed south or take the Port Townsend Ferry to Whidbey Island and on to the mainland."

"They've just veered off to the left, heading for the ferry," the other ranger added.

Grant's patience had run out. "Where are the damn police?" The longer they were in that car, the greater the risk of Kate getting killed.

"I'll tell Flight Service to update the police," the pilot said. "They've joined the line to board the ferry. The cops are parked at the head of the line screening cars as they board. If they got the alert, they'll spot the SUV and keep them from boarding."

"Oh, no!" Grant shouted. "The SUV is pulling out of line and heading back the way they came. They must have seen the police! Stay with them."

"I've got this," the pilot said. "But they can't get far. See the police roadblock? They're pinned."

"They've stopped," the other ranger said. "Someone's getting out."

As they circled overhead, they watched as a gunfight ensued between the kidnappers and the police.

"Oh, God. Stay down, Kate." Grant murmured. "Don't get in the crossfire."

"One of the kidnappers is down," the pilot said. "Why don't they just surrender?"

Grant tried to see, but in their current position, he was on the wrong side of the helicopter.

"There's a woman who looks like she's down too," the pilot added. "Only one man is still standing."

"Can you land somewhere?" Grant asked. "I need to help Kate."

"They've blocked traffic. I can land on the road in the clearing."

"The third kidnapper is on the ground too," the other ranger said. "Police have stopped shooting and are approaching the SUV."

"Okay. Let's get down there," Grant said.

The helicopter was still a few feet off the ground and setting down in the middle of the highway when Grant jumped out and ran. A police officer with his gun drawn beat Grant to the rear door of the SUV on the side away from the kidnappers. Grant could see that Kate and Sam were on their hands and knees on the floor. Kate crawled out awkwardly, followed by Sam.

When Grant ran up to the car, the officer stopped him. "Sir, this is an active crime scene. I have to ask you to leave."

Grant called past the officer to Kate, "Are you hurt?"

"I'm okay! So is Sam. But where are the kidnappers?"

"I think they're dead. We watched the shootout from the helicopter."

The officer put up his hand. "Sir, I'm not going to ask you again. Back away."

"I'm with these two rangers," Grant motioned to the approaching rangers.

"Hey there! I'm the pilot. I reported the kidnapping to the police through Seattle Flight Service. We tracked the vehicle from the air." He pointed to Grant. "This gentleman was here to meet one of the kidnap victims."

"Okay, ranger, but your helicopter is blocking the road. As soon as we clear this scene and remove the bodies, you gotta get out."

"Can we take these two women back to Port Angeles with us?" Grant asked. "They've been through a lot."

"Afraid not. We need to get a statement from each of them about their abduction."

"Not another statement," groaned Kate. "This feels like déjà vu."

"I'm not leaving," Grant announced. He turned to Kate. "I'm staying with you until this gets sorted out."

"You stay here," the pilot said to Grant. "We'll fly to the Port Townsend airport." He turned and addressed the officer. "Sir, could you give these two women and this gentleman a ride to the airport after you get their statements?"

"Sure, we can do that."

"Then we'll fly you back to the Port Angeles airport," the pilot said.

Grant put his arm around Kate's shoulder. "I'm not letting you out of my sight."

Kate was shaking from the close call and all the gunfire. "Thanks."

Grant turned to Sam. "How are *you* doing?"

"It was a close call!" Sam began talking fast and didn't seem to be able to stop. "I wondered if this was it—the end—and if I really might die. Right now, I'm relieved. But what if the cartel is watching us? How do we know if the cartel is going to try something else?"

Grant worried about the same thing. The cartel seemed determined to conceal Cooper's planet-cooling methods and eliminate any interference that Kate and Sam might pose. As he walked with the women to the police cruiser, he glanced at the grisly scene. Three bleeding bodies were crumpled in awkward positions where they fell. It was clear that the cartel was willing to go to great lengths to fulfill their mission, and Grant wondered how they could be stopped.

40

Olympic National Park Headquarters
Port Angeles, Washington

Thursday, July 14 and Friday, July 15

Kate felt emotionally numb and couldn't stop shaking on the police car ride to the Port Townsend airport. Grant gripped her hand and sat close, repeatedly turning to check on her. She sensed Sam's presence on her other side and heard her whimpering, so Kate reached out and squeezed her hand too. Yet all her sensations felt distant and in a fog, as if she were outside herself looking in. Being sandwiched between Grant and Sam gave some comfort and a feeling of containment. Surviving this day, after almost meeting her death, left her grateful and determined to savor every day from then on.

None of the three spoke, and thankfully, the officer driving seemed to sense they needed quiet. The helicopter ride from Port Townsend to Port Angeles was much the same with the two park rangers limiting their voices to the minimum needed to watch for and communicate with air traffic.

Once on the ground at the Port Angeles airport, the three of them thanked the rangers for all their help, and Grant called Ben to reschedule their meeting for later that afternoon so they could get some lunch. Grant ushered them to his rental car and took them to a café in town.

The hubbub in the crowded restaurant was overwhelming with patrons coming and going, dishes clanking as they were cleared from tables, and people talking. Sam's wide-eyed, almost frantic look reflected her jarring transition from months of isolation on the glacier. Kate had no appetite, and the strong, greasy odor of hamburgers and french fries left her feeling nauseous. Grant wasn't eating much either, and he kept looking from her to Sam and back to her again.

Now that the immediate threat was over, the unwelcome and uninvited images of that morning came to Kate vividly: Cooper's confrontation of her and Sam, the struggle over Faisal's gun, Cooper's death, hanging over the ravine, the treachery of her kidnappers, and the deafening gun battle raging outside the SUV. Kate's emotions welled up, and she began crying quietly.

Grant reached out and squeezed her arm. "Let's find someplace quiet where we can all talk."

Kate nodded, her eyes brimming with tears.

Grant paid the check and drove them to a motel just outside of town, arranging for two rooms, one for him and Kate and a second for Sam.

As they stood together in the lobby, Kate struggled to regain her composure. "I need a few minutes before we talk."

"And I'd like to take a shower first," Sam added.

Grant nodded. "How about we get together in an hour? I'll call Ben and see if he can meet tomorrow morning." He pointed toward an open doorway. "The motel owner said we can use this little meeting room."

When Kate and Grant were alone, they embraced and she relaxed into him. Soon she began to sob again, and Grant's tears came too. There was so much unsaid between them and so much that needed to be said. But at that moment, Kate just felt grateful for the closeness and warmth of their being together.

In the shower, Kate washed away all traces of the horrible encounters with Faisal and the phony agent and her henchmen. After putting on the change of clothes she'd brought from the glacier, she felt better and began thinking more clearly. She turned to Grant. "I think it's best if Sam and I meet alone to talk about what we've just been through. I appreciate your offer of support, but Sam just met you. She might be more comfortable with only the two of us."

"Of course. Good idea."

Grant looked so sweet and understanding that she started to cry again.

Kate knocked on Sam's door, and they decided to stay in Sam's room instead of going to the conference room. For almost two hours, the two women talked like they'd been friends since childhood. Their shared trauma had obliterated any barriers that might have existed between them. Tearfully, Sam told Kate how guilty she felt taking Cooper's offers of money and connections to be his lackey in an illegal and unethical enterprise. She also regretted her agreement with Tex to spy on Cooper for the cartel. Kate confessed how her single focus on unraveling Cooper's plot had compromised her relationship with Grant.

Kate shook her head. "My strong personality has allowed me to overcome career obstacles, but it has also cost me my job and put my relationship with Grant at risk."

"I've observed your strength of character. I wish I were more like you."

Kate smiled and took Sam's hand. "You had the courage to warn me and reveal Cooper's plot. I'll be forever grateful to you.

To be honest, I was sure we would die on Panic Peak, and I was terrified in the back of that SUV."

"Oh, me too, Kate. I'm still shaking."

They had both cried off and on, and when they were done, Kate dried her eyes and smiled weakly. "I'm exhausted, but I'm starving. How about we get Grant and find a nice, quiet place to go for dinner?"

"Sounds good." She gave Kate a long hug, which Kate returned.

Their late dinner was infused with soft light from the setting sun through the restaurant window. Green plants in the corners gave Kate a welcome sense of being surrounded by living things after living for weeks on snow, ice, and rocks. The prime rib was exquisite, especially after having eaten dehydrated dinners for days. They talked in soft voices about things in their lives that had nothing to do with the hurt they had just experienced. Stepping outside afterward, Kate felt relaxed, refreshed, and ready to spend some long-needed time with Grant.

That night, alone in their motel room, Kate took Grant's hand. "I want to thank you for coming from Boulder to be here for me today. I will never forget your caring presence."

Grant's eyes glistened with tears. "I nearly lost you. I *had* to be here. And I'm so glad we're back together. Forever, I hope."

Under the sheets that night, Kate felt for Grant's naked body and they made love more tenderly than they ever had before. They slept soundly and didn't wake until they heard the gentle tapping of Sam's knock on their door.

Later that morning at the Olympic National Park headquarters, the parking lot was nearly full with the vehicles of tourists and backpackers streaming to and from the visitor center. Kate wasn't surprised by all the activity. It was a popular park and she'd seen the same frenetic crowds every summer she'd traveled to the glacier. But all this commotion felt overwhelming after the remote, quiet glacier.

Kate told the ranger at the counter that they were there for a meeting with Ranger Ben Johnson. Ben appeared grinning, and Kate felt like hugging him, given their long friendship, but she thought it might look strange to visitors or be shocking to Ben. After he shook Kate's and Grant's hands, she introduced him to Sam. He ushered them through a door to the employee area and down the hall to a small conference room with a circular table. She noticed some streaks of gray in his hair that hadn't been there the summer before. Otherwise, he seemed the same strong bear of a man she remembered, but there was a seriousness bordering on sadness in his eyes.

Ben began, addressing Kate and Sam. "Those were two horrible close calls you had yesterday. How are you doing?"

"A lot better after a good night's rest," Kate said, smiling at Grant and reaching across the table to lay her hand on his. "And Ben, I can't thank you enough for sending the rangers to pick us up. If it weren't for them, we'd have been killed by the kidnappers. How did you know they were imposters?"

"I called the FBI Field Office in Seattle and talked to the real Agent Sasani."

Kate nodded. "The cartel was determined to keep their operation a secret and prevent us from sabotaging their plan."

"Those goons were trying to complete what Faisal failed to do," Grant said. He looked from Kate to Sam. "We should all watch our backs."

Ben nodded. "I agree. And we're investigating how they knew you were flying to the Port Angeles airport. Apparently, their intelligence penetrated our organization. We're working with the local police and the real Agent Sasani to uncover their source. I sure hope it's not someone on my staff."

They all sat quietly for a moment. The idea that the cartel's intelligence had penetrated the National Park Service was sobering to Kate.

Ben broke the silence. "Kate, I asked to meet to thank you personally. You need to know how much your work means to the Park Service and to me. Dr. Cooper's plot forced the closure of the Hoh Rainforest Visitor Center for months. Now it can reopen soon, thanks to you." He paused for a few seconds, then cleared his throat. "I'll never get over watching that family drown in the flood waters of the Hoh River." His eyes glistened with tears.

Kate reached out and squeezed Ben's hand with tears in her eyes too. "You've been so supportive of me and Grant, and you've been a wonderful caretaker of this park and Blue Glacier. I'm so grateful for you, my old friend."

"I wouldn't be sitting here with Kate now if you hadn't contacted me," Grant said. "Thank you."

Ben smiled. "Well . . . I admire you both."

Sam leaned forward and chimed in. "Kate, you taught me an important lesson. I'm going to follow your example from now on by sticking to basic science to solve climate change and not take shortcuts like Cooper and I were doing."

"I'm sure you are aware that the two of you were breaking the law," Ben said to Sam. "You'll have to answer for that even though you saved Kate and turned against Cooper in the end. Agent Sasani will be contacting you."

"I know. I'm prepared to cooperate and do what I need to do. I plan to continue my research once I sort out the legal troubles I've created."

"Grant and I will support you," Kate said to Sam. "The experiment you and Cooper were doing showed promise, but it had side effects and people died. It needed to be done in the open with safeguards."

"Humans have unknowingly been doing geoengineering for the past two hundred years, since the Industrial Revolution, by pumping greenhouse gases into the atmosphere," Grant said. "We've just recently recognized it. Now we've got to get it under control."

Kate turned to Ben. "Grant and I are going to do everything we can to protect our planet. I'm counting on you to take good care of Blue Glacier in the years to come." Kate's voice started to quiver. "I may have seen the glacier for the last time yesterday."

Ben looked a bit embarrassed but said with gusto, "You know I will. And you have important work to do."

With that, they all stood and said goodbye. Kate wasn't sure where her life was headed next or if she would ever see Ben and Mount Olympus again.

Epilogue
Grant and Kate's Cottage
Boulder Chautauqua

Thursday, November 24

Kate had prepared the turkey and stuffing in what was once Grant's cottage, now theirs together. Grant had a fire going in the pellet stove, and the smell of cooked turkey filled the small house. Snowflake slept in her bed next to the pellet stove. An early snow the night before had coated the Flatirons and pine trees on the hills above Chautauqua with a dusting like powdered sugar. This Thanksgiving dinner was to celebrate their being together again. She had decorated with colorful gourds on the dining table, baskets of pine cones in the living room, and a bundle of colorful dried corncobs hanging on the front door.

There was a knock on the door, and Kate opened it to find Sam, whom she had been expecting, standing on the porch.

Sam held out an arrangement of yellow and orange flowers. "Thank you for inviting me."

"They're lovely, Sam. Thank you. Come in."

She took Sam's coat and hung it on the coat tree behind the door before calling out to Grant to let him know Sam was there.

Grant came out of the kitchen wearing an apron and a smile. He reached out to shake her hand. "It's good to see you again. We're so glad you could join us."

Conversation over dinner began with catching up on all that had happened in the four months since they'd last been together.

"Grant, how were you able to extend your stay in Colorado?" Sam asked. "I thought your assignment ended after a year?"

"They liked the results I've had at NCAR focusing on solutions to climate change and helping scientists get comfortable in an advocate role during public events."

"That's great. And what's new with you, Kate?" Sam asked.

"I got a grant to do research at my old alma mater, Colorado School of Mines, in Golden. They've given me my own lab to study mineral-based methods of carbon dioxide removal from the atmosphere."

Sam's eyebrows shot up in surprise. "That sounds a lot like my field."

Kate simply smiled.

"This gives you and Grant the chance to stay together in Boulder."

Kate put a hand on top of Grant's. "Absolutely. And it's one reason for tonight's celebration. What's the latest with your legal troubles?"

"I told the FBI everything about my graduate research under Cooper while at Caltech and how he recruited me to join his illegal project on Blue Glacier." Sam paused and looked down. "I knew our work on the glacier was not sanctioned by the EPA, the Park Service, or Washington State. We broke a number of statutes. But I was lucky. I wasn't charged. I can continue my research and study methods of geoengineering in the laboratory."

"So will you be continuing work in your lab at Caltech?" Grant asked.

"There's no place for me there anymore—not after Cooper and all the illegal stuff. But it looks like I might get to do research here at CU Boulder. They're doing similar work—converting atmospheric carbon dioxide to limestone in the geomicrobiology lab."

Kate pushed her chair back from the table. "How would you like to come work in my lab while you finish your dissertation? Your geochemistry experience would make a huge contribution and fit with our mission at Mines."

Sam's mouth fell open in surprise. "Seriously? I'm amped!" She began talking faster, her voice excited. "I got Cooper's and my computers from the FBI and recovered all my research data and notes. The bigwigs at Caltech say I can move my lab equipment to the school of my choice. They don't want our data either, claiming it's suspect."

"Wonderful," Kate said. "If you can come to my lab tomorrow, I'll show you around."

"I'd love that."

After dinner, Grant said, "You want to go for a hike?"

"What? Now?" Sam asked.

Kate stood with a stack of plates and moved toward the kitchen. "It might be fun. There's a full moon, and we could keep talking."

"I'll grab some flashlights too," Grant added.

After putting on parkas, gloves, and hats, the three went out the back gate of the property to the open space behind it with Grant in the lead. The trail climbed steeply up the side of the hill, giving them a stunning nighttime view of Boulder. They kept the conversation going as they hiked.

"I have been asked by the FBI to describe Tex," Sam said. "Then the CIA called me in to tell them everything I know about

Cooper's formula for blending sulfur in jet fuel. When I met with them, they said they haven't been able to locate any members of the cartel, but all the fuel-screening equipment at airports has been modified to block the sulfur-tainted jet fuel."

"Did you ever get any of the money for your mother's care that was promised, or was that cut off when the cartel's plot unraveled?" Kate asked.

"No. Not a penny. I don't expect to. Good riddance."

Kate decided to change the subject and comment on the spectacular view from their vantage point.

"Boulder is a beautiful city," Sam said. "I'd love to live here."

Grant kept hiking at a brisk pace and Kate was keeping up, but Sam's breathing was a bit labored. Kate said to Grant, "Let's slow down. Sam just arrived from sea level."

They stopped for a moment and Kate turned to Sam. "I also want to share an idea that Grant and I have been discussing for some time. We want to form a consortium of scientists, headquartered initially in Boulder, where a large number of like-minded scientists and research institutes are located."

"A climate scientist at NCAR, Liu Yang, is interested in joining us, and she has contacts at NOAA who would like to be involved," Grant said.

Kate added, "We want to tackle the problem from an interdisciplinary, interagency perspective. We think Grant's approach could foster the coming together of diverse scientific disciplines across a broad community."

Grant took Kate's hand. "The intellectual and emotional synergy might spark the breakthrough that's been missing."

Kate grinned. "We would love to incorporate the work you were doing capturing carbon dioxide in limestone into our search for processes that occur naturally on Earth. What if we could identify and enhance the processes that nature provides so they can keep up with, or even reverse, the buildup of greenhouse gases?"

Sam's eyes sparkled. "We had an encouraging start with our limestone production, but it was never developed to a scale to affect Earth's climate."

"Let's talk some more after we visit my lab tomorrow."

When they returned to the cottage, the three talked well into the evening.

After Sam left, Grant and Kate sat close on the couch holding hands.

Kate was nestled under Grant's arm, looking at the flame in the window of the pellet stove. She marveled at how good it felt to be with Grant. She knew she could be self-sufficient living alone. She'd done that for years before meeting Grant. And when they first lived together in Seattle, she'd worried that her love would make her too dependent on this man. Now, after everything that had happened and how they'd managed through it, she no longer worried about losing her independence. She relaxed and let his love for her permeate her whole being.

Warming World Adventure Series

Watermleon Snow

Panic Peak

Acknowledgments

I was trained to teach and have done so most of my adult life in settings ranging from high school, graduate school, health care, and industry. So when I started writing climate fiction, my goal was to teach about climate change while telling entertaining stories. I wrote *Panic Peak* to inform readers about the technologies being considered to counter relentless global warming.

The seed for my story was planted by the climate scientist, Jadwiga (Yaga) Richter, whom I met at the National Center for Atmospheric Research (NCAR). Her project at the time consisted of using an Earth system model to examine possible effects of geoengineering on the entire globe.

Later I received input from Roy Rasmussen, also at NCAR, on cloud seeding activities underway in Wyoming to increase snowfall. Rajendra (Raj) Agrawal, an aircraft engineer and fellow novelist, helped me understand the possibilities and limitations of using commercial aircraft to cool the planet. Jeffrey Kiehl, a climate scientist who became a Jungian analyst to help people cope with climate change, provided insight on how attitudes about climate can be adjusted. He referred me to a colleague, Andy Szasz who is a strong advocate for dealing with the climate through his leadership in sociology. For another perspective, Dr. Kiehl referred me to Slawek Tulaczyk, a prominent researcher in glaciology, who described his study of shrinking glaciers while communicating the basic science.

My writing benefitted immensely from the careful editing of Laurel Kallenbach, who guided me through the pitfalls of writing a sequel after having edited my first novel, *Watermelon Snow*. She served as a coach to help me continue writing in the face of the COVID pandemic and a period of personal loss. Once the manuscript was fleshed out, Melanie Mulhall provided a fresh set of eyes, helping me identify and smooth out some issues between my main characters, Kate and Grant, and other rough spots.

At various points along my writing journey, I received valuable feedback from Caitlin Berve and fellow members of her writer's critique group in the Boulder Writers Alliance. Also, friends Rodger Stewart, Bob Terrill, Judith Auer, Jeff Modesitt, and my son, William, gave me the benefit of their unique perspectives after having read my first novel in the series. The novelist Margaret Mizushima shared her approach to crafting plot and characters, which helped me keep the threads in my novel from becoming tangled.

My life as a novelist would have been far more difficult without the understanding and constant support of my wife, Nancy, who sadly developed Lewy body dementia while I was still writing the early drafts and eventually succumbed to her illness.

I have no words to describe how wonderfully blessed I am to have a new partner and bride, Cathy, who entered my life after more than fifty years since we dated in college. Cathy has added unique insight to the plot and depth of characters in *Panic Peak* based on her training in psychology and experience with providing couples therapy.

Panic Peak is truly the product of the concern, curiosity, and generous contributions of many individuals in my life, and I am grateful to everyone who played a part in its creation.

About the Author

Bill Liggett writes fiction that blends behavioral and earth sciences in the recent cli-fi (climate fiction) literary genre. His goal is to paint a hopeful future based on solutions to global warming.

He holds a BS in geology and an MA in education, both from Stanford University, and a PhD in applied social psychology from New York University. Among the many positions he has held over the years, he taught in high school and college, conducted behavioral science studies for IBM, and consulted with health care and educational organizations.

Wherever he lives, he loves being outdoors. Home for him has included the West Coast, East Coast, Alaska, and now Colorado, the state of his childhood. He and his wife, Cathy, live in Niwot, Colorado.

www.williamliggett.com